About the Author

A mother of three and a military wife. The author has been studying psychology since early childhood when things started to fall apart. She learned mental health is closely related to nutrients in the body, hormones, and stress. This series is the result. She hopes you enjoy and learn things about yourself you never knew. She hopes those things grow you into the person you were always meant to be. Thank you for choosing her series to spend your time on.

Releasing the Venom

Adeline Grace

Releasing the Venom

Olympia Publishers
London

www.olympiapublishers.com
OLYMPIA PAPERBACK EDITION

Copyright © Adeline Grace 2024

The right of Adeline Grace to be identified as author of
this work has been asserted in accordance with sections 77 and 78 of
the Copyright, Designs and Patents Act 1988.

All Rights Reserved

No reproduction, copy or transmission of this publication
may be made without written permission.
No paragraph of this publication may be reproduced,
copied or transmitted save with the written permission of the publisher,
or in accordance with the provisions
of the Copyright Act 1956 (as amended).

Any person who commits any unauthorized act in relation to
this publication may be liable to criminal
prosecution and civil claims for damage.

A CIP catalogue record for this title is
available from the British Library.

ISBN: 978-1-80439-473-1

This is a work of fiction.
Names, characters, places and incidents originate from the writer's
imagination. Any resemblance to actual persons, living or dead, is
purely coincidental.

First Published in 2024

**Olympia Publishers
Tallis House
2 Tallis Street
London
EC4Y 0AB**

Printed in Great Britain

Dedication

I dedicate this book to my miracles: George, Jonathon, Efthemia and Niko.

Acknowledgements

Thank you to my husband, George, for always being there.

Introduction

Anastasia is a regular suburban stay-at-home mom. She is married to a military man, Dimitri, whom she madly loves. She is raising three toddlers who keep her on her toes and as busy as can be. Though they keep her busy, it does not keep her mind from flashing back to her rough past. Her past keeps pulling her back in as she fights to finally release herself.

Loving her family and being present is her top priority. Put at risk from her CPTSD (complex post-traumatic stress disorder). Every day is one day closer to healing and further away from the everyday abuse of a boyfriend, she held closely. This boyfriend was abusive in many ways and attempted to make her life hard in any way possible.

The story follows Anastasia as she sorts through flashbacks when they come. Meanwhile, she is trying to escape them while she is with her family. She continuously gets caught up in the forced memories while the children are present. Memories that would cause anyone to turn back into the survivor weapon they became to escape such a situation.

At the very least, Chris was a jerk. At the most, he was a murderer. This is left up to the reader to decide as they follow along and answer personal questions throughout this series. Decide whether Annie should have the CPTSD she has acquired. Or she is just weak and calls the flash of memories, which she likens to nightmares, by the wrong title.

Meanwhile, following Annie's day-to-day life of being a

devoted stay-at-home mom and loving wife. Being such a rare breed in a world where most moms were required to work to assist in household earnings. Is Annie lucky to be home or a slave to yet another life she chose? She asks the readers eye-opening questions that may direct them down her same path. Ideally, it will allow them to know themselves enough not to end up in the same abusive situation as she did.

Part One

Chapter One

It's an odd thing, a past that makes you more cautious than you want to be. Always reminding you that there are lines you dare not cross. Flashing memories through your head of times gone by in places, of people, of feelings, even triggers CPTSD is what they call the kind of gift that a rough past gives you.

The love of a narcissistic sociopath wraps around you, makes you breathless and panicked, and drops you into survival mode. That's what Anastasia had: triggers. Everything was a trigger, from the color of someone's eyes to the way one person touched the other. She spent her days analyzing the reality she had created to survive the horrors she had been through. It is interesting to think a whole lifetime could go by and one measly relationship would rip her apart and completely change the person she thought she was.

Yet, that seemed like a lifetime ago, as she gripped at the soil in the farm field her husband had purchased for them. Looking down, she saw her hand caress the warm spring dirt, recently kissed by the sun. She closed her eyes, lifting her chin toward the sky, and felt the same sun kissing her face. Deep breathe in, and then out. Deep breathe in, and then out.

Breathing in the smells of nature as the wind wrapped around her to reassure her, everything would soon be all right. Just a moment ago, she was plagued with a memory. A memory that felt more like a nightmare. She knew she could not run, though she tried. She threw her purple jacket and black sneakers on and ran outside.

She ran so far that she could no longer see her lovely colonial home. The home she shared with her husband and three children. Then she dropped to her knees and grabbed the soil to remind her that this was her new reality. She, more than anyone, knew reality was a fluid idea. It could be molded by someone if you let them in enough.

She knew that even a distance away from her home, she could not escape the reality in her mind. Though she ran, not for herself, so those children and that husband could not see the pain that she was facing. But God already knew, He watched as she failed to listen to Him. As she moved closer and closer to her demons and further and further from Him. Closing her eyes and breathing in one last time (if she was gone too long, they would notice and come for her).

Soon she had the strength to stand once more. She looked up at the blue sky, taking deep breaths in and out. She looked out at the land, the ever-forgiving, ever-producing land. Deep breath in and out. The agony of her memory slowly faded.

She turned around to see her husband and children in the distance, walking toward her. She knew she had to be strong once more. Anastasia did not want them to know or experience the horrors that she had. Smiling, she started to walk toward them. Slowly, she moved, continuing to breathe, as the memory unlatched from her mind.

Soon the kids were in her arms, and her husband was kissing her. "What happened?" asked Dimitri.

Not wishing to inform him of her pain, Anastasia said, "Oh, I just needed to be outside." By this time, Dimitri knew Anastasia had such a relationship, but he could not fully understand, nor was he always in tune.

He smiled as he wrapped his arms around her, and the kids went further into the field to play. They began to talk, and he spoke about trees and plants he wished to put in the ground in the coming months. He spoke with her about the days he would have off from his demanding job. These were things that she could handle, and which helped her know Dimitri was madly in love with Anastasia.

She watched his face as he spoke. I am in awe of his ability to be present and use anything to show his love. Lost in the moment, she kissed his scruffy cheek and wrapped her arms around his waist, pulling him as close to her as possible in her arms and in her eyesight were the rich miracles God had granted her.

Miracles she had given up on ages before Yet God, in all His sovereignty, refused to give up on her and His plan. Anastasia smiled as she heard Dimitri's beautiful voice continue and saw their gorgeous children running and playing together. This was her new reality, right where she was meant to be.

Chapter Two

Anastasia was still a ripe young woman. Her husband, Dimitri, was a few years older and sported the sultry salt and pepper hair she always dreamed her husband would have. He had rosy cheeks and scruff that he had to shave regularly for his career. Dimitri was a serviceman. Spent his entire adult life serving the country he loved.

Anastasia always dreamed of joining the service but could never quite take the plunge. She always ran into people telling her not to pursue such avenues. "Look at your parents; do you want to be poor like them?"

"You would hate the service; it's not right for you." Two of the many things said to her through the years.

By the time she had enough willpower to break past those people and comments, she was too sick to join. Plagued by so much illness, she could not stand for more than four minutes at a time. Another special gift given by a rough past she found so much pride in telling people that her husband served. Anastasia loved Dimitri's drive and passion.

She loved his intelligence and his stories; boy, could he tell stories? Anastasia found herself swooning over him again and again. Almost three years into their lifelong love, he still had stories that she had never heard. Ahh, to be young and in love, to believe that three years is a long time. In her few "successful" relationships, three years were an accomplishment.

But looking at her parents and many couples like them, three years was nothing. Her parents had met and married within three months, and they had been inseparable for almost forty years. *Maybe one day, if we don't give up, Dimitri and I will make it there too,* thought Anastasia out loud. In fact, those last three years felt like heaven to Anastasia compared to her eight years of torture with her ex. Yes, there were highs the size of Mount Everest, and Chris was great at romance.

But the lows took her to the depths of the sea, and most days she felt as though she was drowning. *I tried to swim hard enough to get to the surface but never quite made it up.* With Dimitri, things were different. Dimitri lacked the art of movie-scripted romance. Anastasia never found herself sailing the high seas on a yacht, being gifted a gorgeous dress for a ball he was sweeping her away to, or even going to a fancy restaurant she eagerly wanted to try.

No, Dimitri was more predictable. She never found herself asking where he was or when he would be home because he always spoke with her. Nights he did not have to travel for work were spent sleeping by his side, holding her hand as they slept soundly. Days were filled with spats about staying off your phone and trying to talk over little voices yelling "Daddy!" so excitedly that they would explode if he did not answer soon.

Moments of peace filled her with his arms wrapped around her and his sweet lips caressing her face. Evenings filled with baths, dinner, story time, songs, and prayers Most of which Dimitri rejoiced over and took care of. This was not scripted love by any means. No, this was a true and fulfilling love.

When Before Anastasia was sent to take care of her abuser's family and friends while he took care of whatever business or lady he wished at the time. Now she could finally take care of the family she always wanted-a family of her own that she raised with her partner in crime. Consider what type of love you would rather have: whisk you away and fluid, or steady and constant like the ocean. Usually, the whisking romance was more of a puddle, and when the sun came out, it dried up and was lost.

Yet the ocean took any weather and stayed its course. Deep and strong, it held in the beauties of nature. Life was nurtured and created within its boundaries. Dimitri's love was the ocean.

Chapter Three

Anastasia stared out at the beauty that surrounded her from a comfortable seat in the sunroom connected to her home. As she sipped her cappuccino, it played two roles: the role of keeping her awake and the role of bringing her a delicious treat to remind her that she was doing well. It pushed past her lips, and with each sip, she smiled, thinking how she never thought life could be so sweet. She was surrounded by loved ones who accepted her and all the material possessions she could want. The sunroom served as a playroom for her kids.

It had toys arrayed amongst the cubbies that resided against the walls. Anastasia wondered what life would have been if she had chosen a different path. Slightly irritated by the toys, she stared out day in and day out. Not knowing what else she would fill that space with or her time with if they were not there. Life had been empty before children.

She found she had to entertain herself, look for affection, and seek constant interaction. Children willingly gave these things to her without a question or second thought. If she had stayed away from Chris, would she have had these children sooner or not had them at all? Though the regrets of years lost drove her crazy, they gave her education in areas she would use again one day. Since Anastasia was young, she always had what Christians called a "Servant's heart."

She wanted to take care of people and make their lives better, but she rarely took time to focus on herself. Though there is much beauty in such a treasured heart, with every pro comes a con. Bad people could see her heart a mile away. They felt at ease with the idea that there would be little resistance to abuse. And good people sought to protect Annie and her heart.

The moment Chris told Annie that others thought he was a wolf in sheep's clothing should have been her message to run away. But instead, she chose to protect him. She found herself protecting him again and again. In retrospect, others were right. Chris came into Anastasia's life with promises, and love bombed her into thinking he was a good man, but he was nothing of the sort.

Anastasia continued down the road of thought her mind often drifted to: "Where did I go wrong? When did it happen?" Glimpses of moments flashed in her head. Early on, questions he asked and places he took her to She was so certain he was the one that she ignored the red flags.

Instead of protecting herself and those she loved from him, she protected him. It was not long before he had her right where he wanted her, isolated from her family and friends and feeding into every word he said. Anastasia's mind flashed to one of the first dates they took. He drove her to a rocky pier; at the time, she thought, *How romantic.* It would be years before she knew what his true intentions were that day.

The pier was connected to a giant lake. It was nighttime, and no one was around. As they drove there, he asked if she normally rides in cars alone with boys. A question made her feel like she had to prove herself to him. "No, I rarely am alone with boys at all."

"Good, good." They went on chatting as he drove her further and further away from houses and people. The night grew darker, and she unassumingly kept up with him in conversation. You see, he already knew she was independent and had a bad past with cops, which would make her unlikely to call them. The car stopped, and the lights and engine turned off.

She got out with him. He walked her to the pier, convincing her of his romance. That is what this was-simply romance. Anastasia had never been romanced like this before. He led her out onto the rocks and joked about pushing her in.

Anastasia then revealed she was an excellent swimmer and would easily swim to the shore from where they were. A text popped up on her phone. He was upset and decided to leave her on the rocky pier to go back to the car. She called for him, not knowing what she had done to upset him. Not realizing he was not joking about pushing her in.

He pushed his anger down and, after a moment, turned around with a smile and called for her to come to him. Waving his long arm, he said, "Come on over here. We should be getting you home." Safely back in the car, engines ignited, and lights came on to void out the darkness they had just been standing in. Annie smiled and carried on the conversation.

Chris spoke along with her as he thought of his next attempt to rid the world of her. Not long after, he would total his own car to kill her, and when she was miraculously unmarred (as she saw the car coming and told him to stop, yet she pushed harder on the gas), he became upset. He would spend years blaming her for that truck being totaled, bringing it up when she was vulnerable to such trivial discussions. A story she dares not broach at this time, for she had spent too much brain power on memories that no longer held space in her life. Today, she would breathe her way out before the panic attack started.

Something she learned to do through trial and error. She would reground herself by recalling the things she could touch with her hands and see with her eyes. The faint sound of her kids playing upstairs and the hope of a new breath coming to wash the old one away and bring in the new deep breath in, then out. Eyes on the sky and sun; one more breath in, then out.

A sip of her sweet drink, and the thoughts were forced away by the present, looking at the grass now and the Christmas, tree. *New England rarely had no snow at Christmas yet here we are*, she thought, *forty-degree day in December-no snow, no rain, no wind.* Just sun and blue skies. A New England girl knows to soak such things in in the winter.

The things Anastasia refused to take for granted were seemingly small things, which in reality were huge. A blue sky painted by God for us to stare at as long or as short as we wish. The crisp green grass and the barren trees lining the hills surrounded her country home. A majestic God who loves us, who has saved us through Jesus Christ, and who wants to joy over us, glorifying him. Our God, our home, our present (gift and time), and our lives no longer the past.

Now the present and our whole future are ahead of us. Anastasia embraced the words as they formed into thoughts in her head. The past does not define your present or future but should never be forgotten as it tends to repeat itself, especially evil. Be wary yet carefree, and one day you will trust again. Yourself, God, and others. One day...

Chapter Four

Anastasia hummed Christmas hymns as she prepared her home to wrap presents. The kids tore through the house like a hurricane and left the aftermath that coincided. She picked up each little toy, wondering when she would need to purge again. Anastasia never really cared for purging; in fact, she would be identified more as a packrat. Coming from a poor family, she knew to hold onto the things she needed and loved.

One never knew when they would have enough money to purchase another of anything that became broken or misplaced in the trash. Her father worked very hard, and her mother stayed home to save money and raise Annie and her siblings well. Five kids in all. Each has their own wild and free spirit with a strong mind. In fact, Annie's kids were much like her siblings and herself.

It was not until she got into the toxicity of hoarding, granted to her by her ex, that she realized the extreme beauty of purging. Hoarding is the result of unresolved pain, suffering, and even trauma. But if one were poor enough, hoarding could give a person the opportunity to have all they need and to sell items when they need more money quickly. That is why Chris's mom hoarded, and so did he. Anastasia hated to look for anything, knowing that what could take minutes, if properly organized, would end up taking hours.

One day, when things were going well and Anastasia also known as Anastasia, was under Chris's thumb, he took her to his friend's house. As Dorothy's (a mother of nine who Chris grew up with) grandkids came out to play, Chris decided he would aid them by giving them a toy from his trunk. Outside, he went to his car on that lovely summer day and popped open the trunk. Anastasia became concerned because he was outside for a very long time. As she approached the door of Dorothy's garage, she found Chris with a pile of junk at his feet as he continued to look through his trunk for this toy.

She rushed to him, only to have him yell at her out of embarrassment. She calmed him down and told him, "It's okay. We will find it!"

Rummaging more, she questioned what it looked like. "See, this is why you should not have come over; you aren't even helping. You don't even know what I am looking for. Go away; I will do it." She stood and took the insults. mostly because she had no escape as he had picked her up from her home forty-five minutes from there. Moments later, he popped a fox-looking throw toy with his hand clasped around it. Annie could never truly understand why he kept all that stuff in his trunk.

Once he retrieved it and threw it to the boys, smiles became plastered over their faces. She turned to him and said, "Why do you keep all of that in your trunk? It is a mess. You should clean it out."

To which he replied, "Don't talk to me about this."

And he closed his trunk, then walked away from her, leaving her in his car alone. Years later, she would clean her car, and he would trash it to keep her low and remind her what she was to him: trash. When she became pregnant and contacted him many moons after the fox toy experience, he would ask her over and rejoice over his female roommate taking the time to clean and organize his room. This was to win his favor and have him stay with her instead of moving in with Anastasia. In one area of his life, he never let Anastasia even touch.

Annie knew she would never be right for Chris or for him and it only confirmed her desire to raise Albert alone. She waited to tell him something until she was certain he did not want to be a part of the process. Chris was not ready to be a father or even an adult, and there was no way he would be a good example. Sometimes it takes years for someone to escape the idea that they need to protect and nurture their attackers. They attack because they were never truly loved and need someone to love and protect them.

So, Anastasia spent years running that course. Only to realize she was trying to protect the world from Chris. Then to have her name marred and her whole being destroyed. To become a carcass as empty as the soul of her attacker. She refused to let Chris touch this innocent child with anything other than love and adoration.

Now the person she needed to protect was Albert, and she needed to be whole enough to destroy anyone who came against him. This would take many years, prayers, and processes to set in place. Annie knew she must succeed in this endeavor for the good of herself and Albert. There is nothing like a new life to push another to live again to their fullest instead of spending each day praying for death. Something Anastasia had been doing for years up until the point of conceiving Albert.

Anastasia backtracked. She pulled herself out of the spiraling thoughts as Dimitri begged for attention. Physically moving himself closer to her. She knew she now needed to focus on her husband, who had taken days off just to be with her and their children. The husband, who loved and claimed all the children she birthed as his own, He now had two biological children: Scott and Rosie.

However, she chose to love Albert with all he had and see him as his first child and the one who turned his life around. When Dimitri met Annie and Albert, he was in a dark place in his life. Anastasia knew he was infatuated with her, but when he met Albert, something inside changed. He spent his days playing with Albert and letting Anastasia know that if they could not have children, Albert would be more than enough. Even though Albert still possessed Dimitris personality, they have an unbreakable divine bond.

Dimitri is the only father Albert will ever know. Though Angus and Rose took that place at the beginning of his life, Even on Anastasia and Dimitri's first date, when Albert was a little over a year old, Dimitri pried out of Annie that she had a child. "What are you doing for Valentine's Day? Would you like to hang out?"

These were repeated about three times before Anastasia finally told Dimitri that she would be spending that day with her little boy. This made Dimitri exceedingly happy for many reasons: 1) He knew there was no other man in Annie's life. 2) He knew he could enjoy some time with this son of Annie's if she gave him the opportunity. 3) At the time, he was certain this family was meant for him, so he was excited to meet his son. During that time in life, Anastasia did not know where the path would take her and Albert.

But she felt instantly that Dimitri was her God-sent miracle man. So even now, when she prepared for her quiet time and he did not listen, she was willing to let it slide. It is better to have a happy husband than to take quiet time every day. She knew he would not be around tomorrow, so she could take her quiet time then. Dimitri was low-maintenance in this area compared to

Chris.

Chris took all of Anastasia's free time, and because she willingly gave it, he stopped respecting her. Though Dimitri would push into her quiet/alone time, he certainly needed his own; therefore, he was extremely respectful of Annie's unless he really needed her attention. One more breath before she went to join him. Attempting to breathe out the memories and the present. She knew her near future was to follow Dimitri around and engage in conversation that he would lead.

Engaging in a good man who loved her and wanted to share every aspect of himself with her-that is what he was. Not a little boy who needed all of mommy's attention like Chris. She hoped that even in moments she folded to Dimitri he would find a way to see her needs and respect them and her. Something only time would tell.

Chapter Five

It was another warm day in December. Anastasia worked hard to make her home clean and the little ones happy so she could slip away for a mommy-son date with her oldest when Dimitri got home. She had longed for days like these. Days she would be able to show the children how dates should go and how to be wooed. Dimitri was on board with Anastasia's wild idea and beat her to the punch.

Last week, he took Albert on the adventure he had been waiting for, walking through the woods. Dimitri was, in most regards, a survivalist and loved the outdoors. If he could be outdoors all the time, he would. But work and life kept him inside most days. Albert loved being outside as well.

He fantasized about walking through woods with trees so high that he had to lay on the floor of the forest to see the tops of them. This was a dream that erupted from time to time with Angus in the woods by their house. Anastasia and Dimitri did not live in a wooded area; therefore, Albert could not relive this dream from the back yard. That day was different. Dimitri jumped in the car, picked Albert up, and drove him to one of the local county parks, where there was a wooded lot. Though the gate to the park was locked, he knew they could walk the part of the woods that was bucking the road.

So he parked, and the boys got out to walk. I was now walking through woods that were; to say the least, hairy. Trees that almost fell on them as the wind blew and sticks along the ground that could impale if landed on just right, Albert had a smile that went from one cheekbone to the other. He chatted away with Dimitri, who was also loving the experience but was cautious to monitor Albert's moves and what was around him in case he needed to jump in and protect him. Dimitri's heart was full as he heard Albert's little voice speak to him.

Albert asked questions that Dimitri answered, and vice versa. They both knew that this time was priceless and wanted to soak up every moment of it. Soon Albert was too cold to continue, and they turned back toward the car. Dimitri redirected them as he continued to listen to Albert air his heart out through words. Wishing to extend this time, they went to a local coffee shop and had hot chocolate and cake.

Oh, how he loved to shower Albert with love. Albert was special. Dimitri always wanted children, but his career and past relationships made him believe it was impossible. Then along came little Albert; he was eighteen months old at the time. At that time, Dimitri was trying to release himself from the toxic life he had fallen into.

When he saw Albert's face, everything else seemed to fade. He knew everything he had wanted was sitting right in front of him, by the grace of God, and nothing else mattered. No fears, no deadlines, no one hanging everything or anything over his head. None of it, just the most precious little boy God had given him to steward. Somehow, he must have done something right to deserve that kind of miracle.

Dimitri described Albert as an old English man sitting across from him, breaking bread with him. Albert saw Dimitri as the dad God had graciously given him. His safety, his protector, and a strange kind of love he had always longed for Strange? Yes, strange, as Albert and Dimitri were divinely bonded and had the same personalities.

Some days they adored each other and felt their soul's bond, and other days they could not stand each other. Like cats, Albert would want Dimitris love and rush him with questions and hugs. Dimitri had enough from his day and would remind Albert not to come too close. "Go in the playroom." Other days Albert had enough of his day, and Dimitri would rush him with questions and hugs.

To which little toddler Albert would scream, cry, and yell, "No, Dad!"

Both would be hurt at different times. But moments like this daddy-son date made all those moments worthwhile. Their souls rejoiced (like butterflies in their stomachs) as they chatted over hot chocolate, coffee, and cake. Both felt they were exactly where they were meant to be. The best of friends.

Dimitri knew soon he would have to bring Albert home, and the dynamic would shift again. But for that brief, luxurious moment, he felt the magic Albert brought to his life again. Nothing else mattered to them in this moment. To bond and grow in love for each other as father and son. Albert also felt the magic Dimitri brought.

As the oldest, he always needed to be available and ready to help. As a highly intelligent person, he became overwhelmed easily. But eager to help, he would fight it and keep control and composure, even at the ripe young age of four. He was to be the man while Dad was away at work. Then, while dad was home, things were different.

He could embrace the release of control and did not have to protect or help. He could be a kid again. The moment he walked through the woods with his dad, he knew nothing could touch him and no one would hurt him with his dad beside him. If something bad or scary happened, Dad would handle it. If someone needed help, dad would take care of it.

Oh, the freedom, oh, the release, "Dad is bigger than my fears and troubles. I can tell him anything, and he won't mind." Dimitri and Albert were certainly designed to be father and son. No one could ever deny that.

After that day, when they came back beaming and friends, Anastasia decided she would make sure this became a regular thing in the family routines. Anastasia could see their bond is, was, and will be life-saving for them. The more time they spent together, the better, and this would eventually push them to also see what Annie saw.

Chapter Six

The next day, Dimitri took sweet Rosie on her daddy-daughter date. His eyes glistened while he got them both ready to go out the door. He asked Anastasia where he should take her for their time together. Anastasia replied, "Do whatever your heart desires."

To which Dimitri looked at her cockeyed, then nodded and said, "Okay, Rosie, let's go!"

Rosie jumped up and down and clapped excitedly, then said, "Bye, Mom, I'll go with Daddy!" With that, they were off. Dimitri thought of what he could do as he drove and intertwined it with what needed to be done.

He asked Rosie, "Want to go to the store?"

"Yes!"

Now he had a direction. When they got to the hardware store, Dimitri loaded Rosie into a lumber cart and set off. Rosie giggled and smiled as Dimitri told her to hold on and sped the cart up and down the aisle. He moved in a zigzag pattern. Rosie could feel the butterflies in her stomach as she held on as tightly as she knew how.

Soon they had crossed the entire store into the lumber area. When they arrived, Dimitri stopped the cart and asked if Rosie wanted to get off there, to which she replied, "Yes." Rosie, like Albert and Annie, had a speech impediment. Though they were all working to be better with speech, many people still saw it as extremely cute at the age of two. Dimitri half smiled and found his spirit lifted even more.

At the point when Rosie was conceived, Anastasia and Dimitri were simply dating. It was early in their relationship, and though they were very interested in each other, they had both been severely hurt in the past and moved cautiously. Anastasia found she was pregnant, a gift she told Dimitri she would give him on their first date if God was willing, before he deployed. They had become pregnant just weeks before he deployed, and Anastasia had taken her third positive pregnancy test in front of Dimitri the day he was to deploy to Eastern Europe for eight months.

Anastasia looked at Dimitri and stated that he would not have to be responsible for Rosie because she had already been raising a child with Rose, Angus, and Marie's assistance. She also worked full-time and was just starting to get her feet under her. It would be less than a year before she could put together a comfortable life for the three of them (her and her two babies). Dimitri cried and let her know that she could date whomever she wanted while he was gone. But he would come back and see if she wanted; they could try their relationship again.

This confirmed to Anastasia that he would be present no matter what it took. That moment, she realized she would wait for Dimitri. During the pregnancy, Rosie was immensely connected to Dimitri. If she would not show her face in ultrasound after ultrasound, it only took him on the phone for her to feel free enough to do so. If she started in early labor, all Annie had to do was call Dimitri, and his voice would calm Rosie enough to stay inside.

That deep connection stayed throughout her life. Now, as a sassy two-year-old, he felt closer to her than ever. It was moments like this at the hardware store alone that he knew he had made the best decision to stay and be responsible for her. To claim her as his own, as she already was, and he was adult enough to admit it. He pointed to a few different wood types and asked Rosie's opinion.

She replied, "That one," with her hands by her sides. This made it easier for Dimitri to make the decision. He loaded up the cart and threw her on top of the wood in a place where she could not get hurt. Then they rushed to the cashier before her fussiness got the best of them both. They loaded the truck up and got safely back in their seats.

Dimitri saw Rosie's sweet little face and knew he needed more one-on-one time with her. He asked if she wanted ice cream, "Yesh!" So, he took her to the local McDonald's and got a hot fudge Sunday for them both. Then he took her to a swan park, where they sat on a bench, bundled up, and watched the cars coming and going on the street across the frozen lake and the people ice skating around the lake. This was their first official daddy-daughter date.

They both beamed with happiness as they said goodbye to the cold lake and headed toward home. On the short drive back to the farm, Rosie talked and talked to Dimitri about anything and everything she could think to say, whether gibberish or English. Dimitri replied to the best of his ability and embraced the fact that he had found what opened her heart. He placed a seed in his mind to remind himself he would be doing this at least twice a year as the years went on.

Chapter Seven

Anastasia took Albert to the local diner for mac and cheese. This was all Albert requested for their mother-son date. To get the date right and not be placed in a restaurant that would not serve Albert the mac and cheese, he requested Anastasia pour over the online menus of local restaurants. The diner they chose, Ruston's Diner, located in New England, was the only one that served that dish on Fridays. Albert was overjoyed when he found out he would, in fact, be getting exactly what he wanted that day.

They hopped in the car as Albert started stammering out of excitement to be having Mommy alone and getting his favorite food. She spoke with him as they drove directly to the diner, asking him questions about life: "How was your week? What is your favorite song? Do you still like the color, Green?" Albert answered as he looked forward out the windshield as his seat was center of the car.

As they pulled up, they realized there was not much room for parking, so Anastasia chose the first place that looked like a spot, though it was not marked nor seemed like enough room to comfortably get in and out of the vehicle. They were unsure where the main door was. When they finally found their way inside, the atmosphere was wonderful. The restaurant had a counter that jetted out into the middle of the first room, where customers entered. There were chairs and tables surrounding the counter, and then chairs and tables in what seemed more like an alcove area if customers kept walking.

The walls had paintings of the ocean and what seemed to be a man's lifelong travels displayed for all to see. It was a cozy place, perfect for a little boy and his mom to catch a bite to eat. The waitress appeared from behind the counter and let them know to sit where they would like, and she would get to them. Anastasia chose a seat against the back wall. The seat allowed her to see the entry and exit points of the restaurant in case there was a threat, and it made sure she could not have anyone sneak up behind her or from her left.

This allowed her to take a small breath of relief and focus back on Albert. It had been a trying year as she forced herself to attend restaurants and diners, though she seemed to always have panic attacks at them. It seems these were places where Chris would make her feel the worst and embarrass her with outrageous comments, loud mockery, and overall malice toward her as she tried to sit quietly and eat her food. Overall, she had blocked out the worst reasons as to why she hated restaurants and diner. Though she had come to a part of life where she would have to break that habit of avoiding places Chris marred for her.

Restaurants and diners were not the problem. The problem was Chris, and now that he was gone and dwindling from her memories more and more every day it was time to try again. To grow confident in being wooed by chefs cooking for her and waiters serving her no matter what condiment she may request. Or what utensils or drinks she would need, they would get them in hopes of a tip at the end. Not that Anastasia had ever been mean or demanding at a restaurant, but embracing the fact that she went to be served, not to serve, that was okay.

Seeing the door would give her a chance to examine those who entered and exited. Based on their looks, outfits, actions, demeanor, and where they chose to sit, these things would allude to whether they were dangerous to her and Albert or not. She took regular scans of the room as she sat and ate her egg and olive sandwich. Albert absorbed all the bustle and excitement.

He was overjoyed to get all he asked for. This meant in front of him lay three items: a plate filled with a giant mound of mac and cheese, a giant plate of French fries, and a cup filled to the brim with orange juice. Albert, being spontaneous and experimental, also had ketchup and, to Anastasia's astonishment, grape jelly to dip his fries into. Fries those were slightly crispy and mildly warm. Anastasia assisted him in his endeavor to finish the plate fully.

A doggy bag would certainly be necessary, but she tried to make him eat all he could. As they sat in that cozy, older diner beside a wall painted like an ocean landscape, Anastasia taught Albert manners. "Albert, use your fork and knife to cut the fries into pieces, dip them, then place them nicely in your mouth. Chew with your mouth closed. Keep your elbows off the table.

Say thank you and please to the waitress when she gives you something or you ask for something." Of course, she said this very quietly as she drew closer to him. There were many older people around them who spoke loudly and would not have heard any of her remarks unless they were eavesdropping. Soon they had finished their meals or the pieces they would consume. They went to the counter and paid.

The waitress asked Albert what his favorite animal was as she cashed them out. "Dinosaur!" said Albert, looking down at his shoes. Her gaze followed his to see his new dinosaur shoes. He smiled, and she nodded. "Oh, I see, and you even have the shoes to prove it."

"Yes!" Albert beamed with happiness as he had just stolen Mommy away for a little while. Anastasia saw his delight and decided to extend their date. Albert, when asked, wanted a dinosaur book. So, they drove over to Barnes and Noble to explore their selection.

This was a local chain bookstore that Rose had taken Annie and her siblings to when she was a kid. She loved the big, light, airy atmosphere that collided with the warmth of books and intellectuals. A piece of her childhood she was all too ready to share with her children. As they entered the store, they went to the back wall to find the bathroom. Albert and Annie both needed to go prior to being able to focus on anything else.

It took a while to get to the back wall because Albert was struck with amazement looking up at all the books on display, the toys, and the stuffed animals. Finally, they reached their desired first stop. After they cleaned and dried their hands, they exited and took a left. This was a bit out of the way, but as they left the bathroom, the direction they wished to go was blocked. Anastasia did not wish to engage with the obvious couple, so she took Albert in the other direction, where they found the language section.

Due to Dimitri, Albert and Annie were supplanted into a Greek family and church. However, they knew nothing of the language, so she grabbed a Greek phrasebook to better understand and communicate. Then, in the kids' section, Albert could not remember the last time they had been to this area together. It was before he had siblings, while Anastasia and Dimitri were just dating. Dimitri longed to shower Albert with gifts, so he took Annie and Albert to Barnes and Noble and bought Albert a book and a Clifford stuffed animal.

It took about a year, but it was no longer before that exact stuffed animal was Albert's favorite toy. He could not sleep without Clifford. Though he had completely forgotten where

Clifford came from, it only confirmed to Anastasia that Dimitri and Albert were always meant to find each other. Sitting in the kid's section now, they found a series of dinosaur books. A series that Albert wished to be read to him.

Anastasia read them and teared up in some parts. It was not sincerely about dinosaurs. In fact, the word "dinosaur" was used as a type of code for kids. So, everything the dinosaurs were learning and doing in them were things she encountered daily and tried to teach her little ones. Anastasia beamed while she read, not noticing the disinterest from Albert.

Now he was up and looking elsewhere as Anastasia pushed him to see which book of the series he wanted. Looking behind her, he grabbed a Paw Patrol four-pack of books instead. Anastasia requested the dinosaur book one more time, to which Albert replied, "No." So she surrendered; it was his day. Normally, she would leave with nothing, feeling duped by her child.

Trying to teach him that you get what you go to the store for but not today; the pack was inexpensive, and she had already picked out the phrasebook that she had yet to use until this day. They meandered around the store a bit longer; absorbing the essence, then went to the registers. Anastasia let Albert hand his book pack to the cashier and engaged in small talk. Back to the car to drive home.

"Can I sit in the back, Mom?"

"Sure, Albert, but you have to go through the middle." Albert nodded his head in agreement. He went, climbed over the seats, secured himself, and they were off. Albert tried to talk more to Annie, to which she nodded along and said, "Uhhuh," though she could barely hear him.

Not long after they were pulling into the driveway of their

home. Albert was mildly upset that the date was over, but both parties were happy it happened. For the first time in quite some time, they were able to once again be focused only on each other. Rosie leapt up as they entered the house, yelling, "Mommy!" while running into the room.

Rosie would get her date after naptime. Dimitri had already taken her on her daddy-daughter date earlier that morning. He sent Annie pictures as they went to the store and the coffee shop. It made Rosie feel so special with her; the little things mattered.

Just a hug and a kiss or dancing to a song that led into a show-those were the things that lit her little face up. Brilliant for her age yet still young enough to not let the complexities of life overwhelm her. A lovely reminder that adults put up too many walls and barriers while kids bravely choose not to hide who they are. A trait many adults would spend the rest of their lives striving to get back to.

Chapter Eight

Anastasia worked hard to make Christmas biscotti as gifts for extended family. Angry from yet another challenging conversation with family, she thought back to her lowest point yet. You see, this family member had a son who had a lifelong disease. Something Annie did not understand but had empathy for Because of this disease, the whole family was on edge, thinking it possible that this son could die at any point.

Back when Albert was born, Annie had a similar experience. Only the disease was the sperm donor, and it had infected her mind and heart so much that she spent the entire pregnancy working her way out of the shell mentality she was forced to adapt to. Shell mentality: nothing matters, no one matters, and every day is another day to pray for death. The mentality that comes with constant trauma while she was pregnant, he wanted very little to do with her.

At the time, Annie was worried Chris would attempt to steal Albert, so she was happy he did not come to the birth. However, Anastasia lost her house and car keys. Then there were a series of break-ins to the house she lived in with her parents at the time. So, she ended up screwing the windows to a point a human could not fit and requesting the locks be changed. Chris decided to live in the woods outside the house.

At random times in the night, he would shine flashlights into her bedroom window to keep her awake. For a whole year after she had Albert, Chris tormented her. Punishing her for having him, even though she requested he be present at different times.

In fact, when Albert was six weeks old, Anastasia requested that Chris meet him, as she was certain he was the father. Albert looked too much like him, and the test she gave him to show his cultural background was weighed in favor of Chris.

At six weeks, he refused, saying he was too busy. Then she had another friend, a girl by the same name as her sister, show interest in meeting her bundle of joy. Annie set up a time for her to come, and instead Chris came. This was when Albert was seven weeks old. Chris drove up and entered the house while on the phone.

He expressed to the person on the other side of the line that he had something he needed to take care of. Then I hung up. Anastasia tired of holding tiny Albert with her mom in the other room, listening; she felt deflated. She thought, *This guy literally just said that regarding meeting his son for the first time.* So, the meeting began.

Chris was impressed by how good Anastasia looked and decided to try to hit on her, completely omitting the reason for the visit. Anastasia sat on the couch with Albert and requested that Chris sit across from them on the other seat so he could see Albert. However, Chris sat right next to Annie and put his hand on her thigh. Feeling disrespected, Annie laid Albert down in her place and put a pillow beside him to make sure he could not fall to the ground. Her parents had a dog at the time who had been known to run around the house randomly, and she did not want to risk putting him on the ground just to get stepped on.

Annie requested that Chris not pick Albert up but enjoy some time with him, and look at him, and protect him if he rolls. To which Chris picked Albert up and did not support his head. Anastasia rushed to Albert and grabbed him as he started to cry. Now holding Albert, Annie started trying to work out a plan with Chris, to which he stared at his phone and took a call. Anastasia waited, and Chris (not wanting to share any information with

Annie) kept it short.

Back to her request, "I would like you to think of an hour each week, consistently, and come to hang out with Albert to get to know each other."

Chris said, "Well, I cannot think of an hour each week I could do something like that. However, I could come in the mornings to see the boy."

Anastasia felt more unsettled as Chris went on, "I will take the boy for a few weeks here and there when he gets older." The whole time, I called him "the boy".

Now frustrated, Annie told Chris to just think about her request and get back to her. Chris, also frustrated, took another call and used that as his excuse to head out the door. Anastasia, on edge, took Albert and went to the other room to speak with her mother. Rose was obviously biased but agreed that Chris was not investing in or willing to invest in Albert, calling him "the boy", not listening to any of Annie's requests, and disrespecting her time and space.

It was only so long before texts started coming: "You should have told me when you went into labor." Texts blaming her for how she went about things even though he told her he did not want to be a dad or on the birth certificate. It was at midnight that night that the threats ramped up. She smelled his cologne in her room, even though earlier that day their thirty-minute conversation took place in the upstairs living room and her room was downstairs in the basement. Anastasia feared for herself and Albert.

She would egg Chris on by texting him or posting pictures on social media of Albert, and things would get worse. Thanksgiving came, and Anastasia was very tired, as was Albert, now two months old. So, she went downstairs to bed after saying goodnight to her family. Annie had decided she would sleep with Albert on her belly and chest for a few reasons: 1) Albert rarely slept, and he ate throughout the night. Therefore, Annie sleeping in this manner allowed him to eat when he was hungry. 2) She had a dream, while he was in the bassinet, that she woke up to a dead baby with ears pierced. 3) She sensed Chris's presence in her room regularly, and she knew he could not truly touch Albert if he was in her arms. 4) She knew Chris and his past and knew even he would feel sentimental to see a mother sleeping with her baby in her arms. He slept in his mom's arms a lot growing up. That night, as Anastasia laid down and set up the pillows at her sides to ensure Albert did not fall below her, she thought of the wonderful party upstairs.

Rose, Angus, Phillip, and Tajkia are all upstairs together in a house filled with love. It was after the light turned off and she tucked her and Albert in that she looked toward the door to see a tall man staring through the crack. He stood there and stared for what felt like an eternity. She laid still and held tight to Albert as she stared back at the man. He did not move soon. She closed her eyes and prayed it would go away.

It was always at this time that he would do what he wanted, get it over with, and then leave. Albert was safe, and that is what mattered. Not long after, she started getting texts from random numbers that would vouch for Chris. "I am a mutual friend," an unnamed stated.

"I am his roommate," said yet another unnamed person.

Fake Facebook profiles, and so on. Always in the shadows, too weak to step forward. Then the in-person started again. Like the true stalker he was, it started small. Trees started to go down one day or every few days in the woods beside Angus and Rose's home.

Chris was also making a lean to keep him more comfortable in the colder months. It was not until Annie posted a question about it online that Chris stopped. Eight years on and off. Annie knew she should have seen the signs. Chris always needed to know where she was.

He tried to alienate her from her family and only let her hang out with select friends. The first day she invited him to her house, she thought he had left. Having residual fear from Kenneth sneaking through her closet and scaring her for his own entertainment, Annie always checked the closet before she jumped into bed. Most days, the closet was empty. However, that day, she smelled her boyfriend and felt a person in the closet.

She ran to her bed and closed her eyes tightly, hoping it would go away. That set the stage for their whole relationship. When she went to tell him the next time she saw him, he was elated to hear her say she thought it was his dad. This is obviously not what Annie thought. She was testing the waters with it, and him going along with it to get himself out of the position should have told her all she needed to know.

Chris thought, *Finally, I have found a girl willing to believe my lies.* Annie was not worried about dying. She used him as her "safety," even though he was obviously the enemy. He finally found the subject he had been looking for, and he would enjoy every minute of this. Eight years is what Annie gave him. In those eight years, Chris tried to kill her multiple times, stalked her, love bombed her, and abused her.

He manipulated her to the point that her dream state was her normal state, alienated and isolated her from the people who could or would help, and trained her to be the machine he wanted and needed. He cheated on her profusely, blamed her for every single thing he had done wrong, and loved his little puppet so much that he kept her in a mental and emotional cage. Those were the days she regularly ended up on the ground in a ball shaking and crying.

Chapter Nine

Anastasia was twenty-five and dating a new man who was scarier than Chris but, in many ways, nicer. It was only a short time before they both realized it would not work. Annie knew he was not actually leaving for home but decided to go through the motions and act as though he were. The day he left was miserable, and that week was not much better. Rose ended up in the hospital on Christmas, and Angus cried more and more.

It was extremely rare for Angus to cry, especially to be seen crying. He had been laughed at once for it, and he tried to never cry in front of anyone again. Annie did not know what to do, so she turned to Chris. She got them both extremely intoxicated by the mixed drinks she made herself and enticed him to sleep with her. It was a strange time.

There was no conceiving that night. The next morning, Annie called her boyfriend, who had "gone back to his country," and told him what had gone on between her and Chris—all of the details. She knew he would string her along, stating he was being true to her even though he had not been true to their relationship within the two and a half months they had been seeing each other regularly. She did the only thing she knew how to do—played his game. In the moment, she felt the need to beg for him back after breaking it off. He denied her.

She had spent too much time embarrassing him. Annie let his family know she messed up and left it at that. The next week, she went to Chris again, got him drunk again, and gave him his birthday gift. His birthday was December twenty-eighth. It was at that time that she became pregnant with his child.

Something she was told was nearly impossible, and if she did get pregnant, she had an extremely high likelihood of miscarriage. It was late January when she had unrelenting nausea. This was unnatural for her since she always felt sick, and it rarely came to this intensity any more. So, she took a pregnancy test only to find it positive. Then two more, just in case it was wrong. It was not; Anastasia was finally pregnant.

Overjoyed at this new information, she sought to learn everything about being good to her new baby and how to keep it alive and well inside of her until she could have him in her arms. It was a few weeks later that she told Chris. He picked her up to take her with him on his work run. At the time, he dropped off medicine at group homes in the southern region of the state. Annie took that chance to tell him about her happy news.

At her own work a few weeks later, she felt a cyst burst and feared it would ruin the baby, so she rushed to urgent care. Anastasia did not know if the baby was in the protective sac yet or just a zygote still multiplying cells prior. The doctor told her she was pregnant, and she can get checked at the hospital to make sure it is not an ectopic pregnancy. At the hospital, Rose called and begged her to tell her where she was. "Mom, I am fine, I will be home soon."

"No! You tell me where you are."

"Fine, I am in the emergency room at the hospital."

"What! Your father and I are coming."

They rushed to Anastasia and found out she was pregnant. Then Rose pushed Anastasia to get an OBGYN and see them regularly, which she did. She held her hand through the whole process, saying, "If the father will not be by your side, then I am the father." Years later, Annie would tell Rose what happened piece by piece.

She was scared to tell the entire story at once, as Rose was protective. Especially when it came to her children, Annie loved them and certainly had become accustomed to them. Dimitri had that same gift, which Annie rejoiced in.

Chapter Ten

"Physician, heal thyself." Anastasia heard a voice through the thoughts in her head as she drove and prayed to recover from the holiday that seemed all too demanding. Blessed and plagued, she felt. Blessed to be surrounded by so many people who "loved" her and plagued to figure out how to extend love to them in a time of life that seemed too exhausting for such delicacies.

What is love? she thought, *there are so many examples of "love" and so many people confessing their love that the confession of love felt lighter than it should. How did Anastasia love others?* She tried to liken herself to her mentor, Jesus Christ, always in and out of her devotion and worship to Him. And, of course, imperfect, unlike God on earth, whose name is Jesus Christ.

Anastasia saw love as community and support, and she knew her many failings well. Constantly attacking herself for even standing wrong in the company of others, showing too much emotion, or being too vulnerable. Trying to correct herself before anyone else could Anastasia learned love and faith early on in life. When she went through trials, faith felt unattainable.

Thus, love was simply a figment or an illusion, much like how she saw her life today and her past. Simply an illusion, because who could or would allow themselves to go through what she went through for perceived love? Who would take the lashings and abuse the many challenges to their life and closeness to death, though never really death in the physical sense? Who would be caged for the one they loved?

Not just Anastasia, but many. Though Anastasia clung to the wrong love through those years. She worshipped a human as God. Unlike the men and women who worship the true God with their lives. The disciples, apostles, and martyrs who came before her all likened themselves to Jesus.

God, who came down in the form of man to show, guide, and lead people to His heavenly counterpart, became the spotless lamb. Jesus was abused in all forms, caged, and killed for His love. He went through immense trials even before his end because of his love. Not His love for Himself (the Heavenly part), but His love for us imperfect people. To give a new life and hope.

To restore the chance to join Him once again in heaven. Serving humans with His days and His life. That is love. Not presents, not the passing "I love you" with nothing backing it. Nope, love is deeper.

Love is time, devotion, energy, investment, servanthood, and selflessness. Giving up the things that do not benefit those you surround yourself with. We cling to God to grow and learn what He wants for us with those He has put in our lives. To have people around who truly invest and to truly invest in others. There is nothing like American love today, which is a fleeting thought; now you see me, and now you do not, like an illusion.

"God is love." He has come to the hearts and minds of men and women all over the world through the Holy Spirit. Though alone, they may look crazy, but they have banded together over time to write down divine pieces to be read and shared. Writings from God Himself to His people some have used their lives to analyze and better explain these divine writings to the rest of their communities.

Those people who are willing to take the time to hear and

understand. This is the Bible. These are Christian people. The only master we serve that has the power to heal and prosper is God. Let us realize what we have been through is not an illusion but a reality, like God.

In fact, the illusion of fear and the need to stay in the muck because it is the "best" option should be let go and dismissed instead, the reality is to seek and find help. It is best to start reconditioning the abused and marred mind and heart as soon as possible. Servants of the Lord who are abused in the service of the Lord for the people of the church. Though they believe they can do whatever they please to you with no ramifications, God will deal mightily with them.

Justice will be served, and there is no need to burden yourself with these people, as they will only hurt you. Instead, let those abused bind together and serve the true God and His people. Let us heal ourselves in Christ and power forward, working to renew so that we may be more useful for those who truly seek God and the path to Him. Anastasia sat as she listened to the speech coming through the radio after her time of prayer. Soaking in the scriptures references "1 Corinthians twelve and thirteen, segments of the book of Acts, Romans 5:3-5."

Steadfast and patiently waiting on the Lord, praying without ceasing. Thoughts flooded her mind. She tried to push them away to focus on the speech that reached her heart, as she was actively working on healing and attempting to recondition her mind and heart. Forced to think back to those times she felt caged. Those moments of abuse felt like they would never end.

The person sucked the life out of her, yet she willingly went back and took more. Taking moments away that renewed her, so when she came back, he looked at her with hungry eyes, excited to suck more life from her. He must have what she has and must forcibly take it by any means possible. Anastasia knew that going back to what she saw as her addiction, Chris, would only deplete her more and more. He would bring nothing of benefit to her.

He would use any tactics to destroy her and all that she loved. Though he tried to kill her, he could not. Anastasia mourned the others who were not so lucky. Instead, he would make a mockery of her and take all she had from her. That is why she could not marry Chris after she became pregnant.

He even became jealous of the baby, and while she was near him during her pregnancy, he would attempt to kill the baby with pressure, high-stress situations, and overall toxins he would find ways to put into Anastasia's system. There were subtle moves that many would not necessarily catch on to, but Annie had known him too long not to know what his end goal was. She refused to let him take her baby away from her. She let him take her life, family, and friends for years. Anything she loved or cared about more than him.

He forced her out of jobs and into groups and social situations to make her look like a fool. So many tears she cried, so much sickness and death she faced. No more would Anastasia enter a room uncertain of what she would face, always knowing she would be degraded more. No more would she walk into a room where people had had sex with her boyfriend or were currently messing around with him. No more would she be put in life-threatening situations, and she certainly would not let Albert go through such things if she had any say.

No! Instead, if every man was like Chris, she would only love Angus, God, her brothers, and Albert. She decided to use her life to restore and rebuild, to be the best example possible for her son. To put strong, good men around him and show him what good people were like—godly people. Not perfect, but striving to be more like Christ and less like the world.

Albert would not be marred by Chris. Albert was Annie's shining star and last hope. As she sits on her couch across from Dimitri and breaks back into the room, she realizes there are still good men outside of her family. Men who are not perfect strive to love and care for their families, as it is a life goal to be family men. For Dimitri, it was his greatest goal.

Albert not only saved Anastasia the day he was conceived and found out, but he also saved Dimitri. Chris had no concern for him and wanted him dead. But Dimitri rejoiced in the life of Albert. The first day they met, Dimitri fell in love with Albert and knew he was meant to be his son. Even if Albert were his only child, he would be satisfied.

Albert's presence gave Dimitri a reason to live again—a purpose. To leave his manipulative relationship completely, write off his abusive boss, and forge toward a better life. Anastasia watched as Dimitri's demeanor changed. He was finally able to become the man he always wanted to be. Anastasia's reaction to Chris's reaction to Dmitri's reaction meant the world.

He felt about Albert as she had. As she stares at her, now a little weathered, Dimitri can hear small noises from their restless children. Three kids sit quietly on the couch, overwhelmed by their blessings. Anastasia calls Dimitri, Albert, Rosie, and Scott her four miracles. "I went through all of that to get here. And these people this speech is talking about can too.

Lord, if there is a way, please help me help them through my stories. Please build an understanding community around each of us and hold these men and women in your hands. Only you, God, can save us from ourselves, those who have hurt or broken us in more ways than one, and this evil world. Please guide our hearts and minds and save us. I know this suffering may not glorify you as Paul and David did in your word.

Please help us to learn to glorify you through our suffering and pull us away from our abusers and into you. Please give us hope and strength to follow through with what you have for us. We praise and worship you, God, amen." Anastasia and Dimitri held hands and prayed together as she cried healing tears and heard the whisper once more "Physician, heal thyself".

Chapter Eleven

Anastasia sat across from Dimitri as they ate what Dimitri liked to call their cheesy bread. It was a recipe Dimitri made up: bread with olive oil, butter, garlic powder, and onion powder, topped with a layer of cheese, and toasted to make it all melt together. Each bite was delicious. Anastasia loved the taste and the healing factor of his little Greek concoction. She smiled as Dimitri went on about regularly visited topics: work, social and political climates, history, etc.

Embracing the love of a man who wanted nothing more than her presence, focus, and time was hard for Anastasia to wrap her mind around. This is the perfect specimen of a man sitting in front of her in the home he bought, providing for her every need and desire, and all he wished for in return was her presence. Anastasia has never felt that love from a man before. Only from God and her parents. The boys wanted so much more; they were so eager to use her that she felt like the Department of Motor Vehicles said, "Take a tab with a number."

After a while, she only let certain people use her. Only the ones who could truly win her heart. Before Dimitri, the only one who took that place was Chris. Eight years ago, Anastasia sat at Chris' beck and called, "Do this. Go there. You are not fast enough. Why are you not already here?" Chris liked to play what Annie called fuck-fuck games. A common military term for mind games. One day, amidst this eight-year reign over her heart, Chris decided he was going to play with Annie.

Looking back now, she thought he likely woke up bored and said, "What will please me today?"

She came home to her parents' house and went to Rose's room to speak with her. As she sat down, she received updated texts from Chris about when and where to meet him. It started with, "I need you here in an hour dressed for a funeral."

Five minutes later, "Actually, I need you here in thirty minutes as we need to take my bird to the vet together; he has been sick."

It was somehow her responsibility to go with him. Annie continued to talk to Rose for a bit. The next text arrived, "Why are you not here yet?" two minutes after the last. Anastasia felt the stress and quickly got up and apologized to Rose for having to end the conversation so abruptly.

She ran to her room, dressed for the funeral, ran to her car, and started speeding toward Chris. You see, reader, when you start to panic in accordance with your mood swing abuser, there is no stopping the panic unless they bless you to calm down. If Anastasia took one wrong step, she would be blasted by Chris in whatever way he decided that day. Of course, in her mind, she was rushing there to help and be there for him, his bird, and his family.

She did not even consider the fact that she was rushing there at the risk of her own life. While having a panic attack, it was very unlike for Annie to consider herself in this regard. She was very focused on serving the ones around her and neglecting her needs. Though Kenneth tried to teach her and Marie to be better at such things, it took an extreme amount of focus. Which Annie rarely afforded herself?

Just stacked on more people to care for. A normal person would have told Chris to go alone and let the pieces fall where they may. *Not Annie*; she thought she could control the world yet felt she had no control at all. Usually, Chris used complete silence to punish Annie for a few weeks after whatever incident, as she poured into texts apologizing to try to make him come back. Physical abuse had no effect on Anastasia.

Though Chris had tried in the past, Anastasia refused to let him hold any ground in that area. She was a very good fighter and would not let anyone beat her down without paying for it. Chris decided after a few good blows that he did not want to pay, so he chose another angle: the mind and emotions. This was even more fun because he could leave deep scars and bruises that no one else could ever see. It just made her look crazier while her physical body remained the same and her mind and emotions started to destroy her from the inside out.

He would use the things she loved against her and punish her for not "loving him correctly," though he refused to outline such things. Every minute was different, and though she tried, she always failed to love him accordingly. Anastasia was now on the highway to Chris's house in full panic attack mode. Nothing mattered more to her than making it to Chris. Another driver, who must have been having a bad day, decided he was going to cut Annie off and hold her back.

He drove between the two lanes so she would not pass him. Then she flicked her off when she finally did pass him. Annie proceeded forward, her heart racing faster now that her breathing was shallow and rapid and her speed was thirty miles over the normal allotted overage. Into his neighborhood, she went rolling through the one-stop sign she would encounter and was now sitting outside his house that he shared with his mom. She threw her head down, unable to think, after she parked and started to try to take deep breaths.

She knew she could not let Chris see her like this. In her head at the time, it was so he would not worry. But in fact, he usually smiled and embraced her in this state because he knew he caused it which made him proud. Moments later, she looked up and started to look around to see that he was not even home. Annie called, but Chris did not pick up.

Then, five minutes later, he slowly drove up, not even acknowledging Annie until he parked. He walked slowly to her car and said, "I need to go get dressed and get sunshine." Twenty minutes later, he came out dressed and with the bird. All the while, Annie sat in the car, waiting patiently for him.

She was not allowed into their house. He made excuses like "My mom would not like that; she is a hoarder" and so on. Anastasia is trying to calm herself down. She was still convinced she was doing the right thing to appease her boyfriend. Chris came out, walking slowly, and informed her they would be taking her car because he needed to save gas, which she should understand.

He put the birdcage in the back of her car before she had a chance to respond. When she pushed back, he exclaimed how the birdcage was already in her car and how much of an imposition it would be to change everything up now. She looked at her gas gauge and told him she was on ¼ tank. He stated, "You should be fine. Mine is on E. So, this is the better option. Now let's go, or we won't make it.

Anastasia started the car back up, and they drove to the veterinarian. They sat waiting, waiting to be called in. Annie asked about Chris's day, and they had a nice conversation, though he did not ask about hers. Then they both went silent and waited a few more minutes before the veterinarian called them back. She turned to notice he seemed relaxed, and she started to calm down knowing she had done, well and was unlikely to be punished.

The veterinarian checked Sunshine out and let them know he had an upper respiratory infection. Chris acted concerned, and they brought the bird back to his house before they went to the funeral for Chris's adoptive brother-in-law. Chris again chose for

Annie to drive her car to this event that had been in the same direction as the veterinarian yet was further. Every once in a while, he would reward her for driving by filling up her tank, but that had become a rare occurrence. The funeral was a few towns away, in a funeral home situated beside railroad tracks.

The funeral was for a man who had a heart attack while working out on the treadmill in his basement. Anastasia had met the man a few times but never truly connected with him. The day he died, Chris and Annie rushed over to console his wife and three stepchildren. The entire family was at his house within the hour of his death. The coroner came to a full house, and as he took the body out, the adults forced all the kids into a room that did not face the path of the coroner.

He so desperately wanted to set his family up for success. Rich was his name. He did not know he would die so soon, nor did his wife. Though he died sooner than they had hoped, he taught the boys how to be presentable gentlemen, and he set his wife up for success financially. It would be a few years before his wife, Melody, would remarry for the third time.

Her next husband was a military man who gave her two more children and did not have any heart issues. Though Annie had a creeping suspicion, Melody wished the tables had turned and her first husband would have been the survivor instead. He was the one she truly loved. Anastasia thought of Chris as her first husband because he was who she lost her virginity to and devoted such a large part of her life to. She rejoiced that they never got married and saw that as a huge gift he gave her.

When Dimitri came along, she knew he was the only man she would allow herself to marry. Even on their wedding day, she cried inconsolable tears. Though she was scared he would become like Chris, she had to try. She knew this was her one true shot at happiness. High risk, high reward.

Zoning back into the man she took the plunge to marry and

do life with, a commitment she refused to take lightly. A smile crossed her face, the ever-slight curl of her outer lips, and butterflies took flight inside. Annie's eyes locked on Dimitri's; she knew she had made the right decision. Though neither of them was perfect, they both deeply loved each other and wanted to heal and grow with each other. In fact, to both, presence was everything.

God and each other's presence alone healed the wounds inside. Dimitri spends most of his adult life alone due to military service, and Anastasia is in a relationship with a sociopathic narcissist for most of her adult life. Always surrounded by people but feeling completely alone and abandoned most days. In this type of relationship, a person must abandon all they love, even themselves and God, to survive. It feels like no one understands.

Thus, Anastasia left and decided to fight to heal those like her. Then she went to work for an insane asylum to feel the presence of people more like her than she would ever let them know, protected amongst her people. The type of person her ex, Chris, made her become with his love. Yes, Anastasia and Dimitri understood each other on a level that needed no words. They needed and loved each other not only for each day but for a lifetime. But because just sitting in each other's presence was more healing than anyone outside would ever know or understand.

Chapter Twelve

"Finally, a sitter I like!" raved Anastasia to Dimitri. "Not only me, but the kids and the chickens. She seems more like our speed and like the kind of person I like." Dimitri nodded along while Anastasia excitedly spoke.

Then, for the pause in her outward analysis, he said, "Whatever makes you happy, my love." Anastasia had learned to analyze thoroughly when choosing people. She also learned to not read a book by its cover. This babysitter was tough like her on the outside, like she had a challenging life. But she had a good heart and was proper in the company of men and women.

So many people try to find ways into the home to destroy it. Like Satan, isolate and destroy. Though this babysitter did not come to fruition, Annie had been wrong about her desire and need for the work. She had been blinded by the fact that this woman was not trying to flirt with her husband because the others had tried. This always made Annie insecure, and she would choose the one who did not flirt with him every time over the one who did flirt with him.

Anastasia grew up in a home that Satan tried to divide and conquer too many times, using each family member's fears and vices to divide the others from them. However, she was the youngest, and by watching from the genesis to the exodus of each episode, she figured out how to devise the things that would break her family and the things that would not. Anastasia knew, especially after Chris, to trust her instincts and be honest with herself and others in the moment. People do not always know the whole truth, nor is their honesty always honest to the full picture.

If a person seeks to be as honest as possible in each moment, they are striving toward the whole truth. If Anastasia did such a thing and those around her did the same, then she would be able to live a better life and give her family and friends what the world refused to deliver: honesty. Those who have struggled through in-depth moments with dishonest people will feel the weight of this gift. Others may not choose to accept such terms. But each person must choose their own path, a path they will be held responsible for answering in the days to come.

Anastasia wanted no more regrets in this manner. It was the deepest part of Annie's state of illusion. The world Chris had created for her to live in. She denied all ideas that she could or anyone else, but Chris could be right. She only trusted his words.

Her sister started to work with her on this as Annie coped with what she had always run toward—to put her head in the clouds and adapt when times became challenging. Anastasia worked with Marie and her college professor on bringing logic back in. She realized emotion is the main weapon of Satan and those doing his work. This time, she had no conversations with Chris that were honest and logical. She would say something definitive, "Mr. Martin had a green van at the time" (an addition to a story of their conjoined pasts).

But it was not right for Chris; he wanted Anastasia to believe she was always wrong. "No, they never had a green van; it must have been tan." Not that Chris cared or knew at all, just that he had to be right and push Annie further from her instincts. So, he could continue to reign supreme. Marie hurt seeing Anastasia in this state.

She asked her what logic was, which Anastasia could not

answer. Annie's professor, Bob Slebodnik, worked to define that term in the three classes of logic she took with him. His work was integral to getting Annie out of her mindset based on illogical emotion. A person's mindset afforded no space or peace for years. Marie then tried again. "Annie, I see you are struggling. Today, I want you to tell me what is real around you. What do you see?" Annie did not know what to say.

Marie interjected while she touched items in the room: "Here is a table you can see and feel. Over here is a brown chair; it is made of wood."

She went on, and Anastasia started to understand. Look at facts, not emotions. *I do not need to know how the table and chair make me feel, just that they are there waiting to be used. Not to move or sway unless moved by another force*, Anastasia thought as Marie went on.

"Annie, what I want you to do is, when you get in this state, open your eyes to the things around you. I want you to touch what you see and bring your mind back to the real and logical. Touch the chair, touch the table and think about what they are made of and how they hold you or your food. Let the other thoughts fade. Take deep breaths, and you will bring yourself back."

Anastasia started this practice. Multiple times a day, she would start to panic, consumed with fear and emotion. Then Marie would find her and start the exercise. "Okay, Annie, what are you on? On the floor, you are in a ball and crying. Start to breathe. Deep breaths. Look at the floor. Is it clean? Can you see crumbs? Feel your hands on your legs; are they warm and comforting or strong and hurtful? Are the tears running down your face warm and salty? Are they flowing quickly or slowly?"

Marie sent so many questions Anastasia's way that soon she forgot why she was curled up shaking and crying on the ground.

Multiple times a day, at first, until she was able to create her own questions to break out of the fog and touch the things around her that were as real as her. After she learned to break out of the fog, it became a quicker and more controlled process.

Today, Anastasia does this almost seamlessly. Her mind will get triggered, and she will physically feel herself drifting into a memory. Sometimes she lets herself relive it, and other times, when she feels weaker, she will start Marie's process right when she feels the bad memory coming to torment her. Much like the day she ran outside, away from her family, to smell the breeze, feel the sun, and touch the dirt. To look around, away from her eyes, she did not want to see her pain and bring herself back from those ever-invasive and demanding memories.

Chapter Thirteen

Anastasia spent the night out with Marie and her special friend. They went to drink a little and go to the arcade. Anastasia refused to sleepover, so she drove home after sobering up. Leaving Marie around midnight and taking on the almost two-hour drive home. She had fun but felt exhausted within a few hours and just wanted to be home with her family, the purpose of her world.

The next morning, she woke up to a grumpy Dimitri, who stayed up until twelve-thirty a.m. because he thought Anastasia would be home and then went to bed when he realized that was not the case. Dimitri stayed grumpy and Annie stayed tired as they worked together to keep the kids happy, safe, and taken care of. Soon it would be their naptime. It was time for Anastasia and Dimitri to do what they liked and wanted. Dimitri decided to go out of the house and do the grocery shopping and other required chores to maintain an organized and happy house.

It was not until he left that Anastasia could sit down and relax more, knowing no one needed her for at least a little while. Though she held him back from leaving by sharing some songs that expressed her feelings in the moment and then going on a rant about old cheerleading stories. Dimitri could not be less interested in the cheer stories, but he enjoyed the two songs Annie shared with him. Anastasia's cheer days were quick and effective. Her goal was to stay out of the house and get rid of her anger in an effective way.

What better way than intense exercise followed by throwing human beings in and out of the air? She did not like a lot of aspects of the sport. Mostly the cattiness of the girls and their mothers. She also did not like the politics of it all or how close the girls liked to sit and be. By that time, Anastasia and Marie realized they did not like uncontrolled touch.

Both were taken advantage of in the past due to their beauty and pleasant demeanor. It was, in fact, offensive for anyone to put their hands on them or get too close. So, they found ways around it by listening to their music on long bus rides and by exploring competition venues instead of sitting with the other girls until they absolutely had to. Not that they did not like the other girls, just that they felt they were from completely different worlds. Only Anastasia and Marie could understand, as they came from the same family.

The other girls came from challenges in their pasts, but the challenges were comparably different. It's funny to think about how cuddly Anastasia was with her kids now. She spent moments holding each one and telling them how precious they were to her. Mostly going like this: "You are gorgeous, brave, courageous, strong, brilliant, caring, compassionate, and helpful (for Rosie, Annie added, you are dainty, lovely, and elegant)." Then, "Thank you for being our child; we are so proud of you and love you so much, and so does God."

In the evenings at bedtime, she would hold them as she prayed over them. "Thank you, God, for our child (insert name). Thank you for all the gifts you have given them and all the days and moments you have given them to us. I give them to you. Please help us to be good stewards over them and to hold them with an open palm. I ask for their salvation and a cleansing of sins. I pray that you will heal and protect them from head to toe, inside and out, mentally, physically, spiritually, and emotionally, and that you will show them their purpose in their dreams. I pray that you will give them peace, God, and teach them how to glorify you and use them as conduits for your kingdom."

Almost every night Annie would plead with God via this prayer she felt He put on her heart. The kids grew confident and unafraid of touch, but only time would tell if that would hold. *Only God knows*, thought Anastasia.

Raising confident, capable children was Anastasia's main charge. At the bare minimum, she wanted to keep them alive but knew that ultimately, no matter how hard she tried or how tightly she held them, she would not make the final choice in that regard. She had seen far too much death and knew God was always at work and had a plan for everything, especially the ever-painful circle of life. It seems when a baby comes into the world, everyone is filled with so much joy and excitement while the mother toils in pain. But when anyone departs this world, no one feels the weight of the physical pain, just the sadness in their heart and the pull on their spirit.

Though many see the beginning as always bright, the middle as the journey that needs to be remembered and the end as dark. It is in fact, a struggle through life as a whole. It is a physical, mental, emotional, and spiritual struggle, and each day is ours to wake up and choose who or what to give it to. Do we dwell on the pain and misery the world offers? Or do we simply give all our worries and cares to God as he requests in His Word?

For every person, it is important to know you have a choice at each moment. No one can make your choices for you. If you give someone else power, then you will not be able to stand alone when they are gone (codependence). Most of the population will abuse the power given to them, as today there is an isolated, egotistical, psychopathic, and narcissistic society that is being created. So, take the power back or give it to God. and your life will greatly improve.

Chapter Fourteen

It was the end of December, and the weather felt tropical. Rain instead of snow in the New England countryside and grass as far as the eye could see. The trees were still bare from the leaves falling earlier that winter. But the parsnip started to grow on the farm. If a person watched out their window long enough, they could even see the sunshine through the clouds as the blue jays danced and played on the brown branches.

Anastasia took a walk around the perimeter of her yard, as she had grown accustomed to doing. This had two points: to pray over the land and to show force and examine the land as a form of protection. Anastasia learned this was an important thing to do after past challenges. When she was twelve years old, she would walk her dog around the yard in the morning at Rose's insistence. She hated it at first as she stepped into the outdoors, which felt cold on the first step.

But after a few minutes, always felt warmer and more majestic. To say Hercules loved it was an understatement. He would tug at the leash as they walked, hoping to get ahead as fast as possible. Hercules was such an odd dog. He was extremely wolf like in looks and tendencies.

Though when Angus and Rose bought him for the family, they were told he was a mix of border collie and dachshund. He looked more like a black timber wolf. As he grew, even his tendencies to beg made him look like a wolf, ferociously hungry and willing to do anything to get what he wanted. It was not until his older brother, Ian (a morbidly obese Scottish black lab), taught him to beg that the family would dare give him any scraps off their plates. Day in and day out, Anastasia and her siblings were urged to walk with Hercules around the perimeter of the yard. That was one of the times Annie felt safest.

Though her parents did a great job of protecting them. Today Annie walked while thinking of those times with a smile. She looked around as Hercules did and took a deep breath through her nose to peg any inconsistent smells that might lead her to know something was amuck. Praying as she scanned the land, God blessed her to steward over it. Then she thought back to a few nights prior.

She sat with Marie and her friend as they ate their food and felt a strangely familiar presence. She looked to her right to see a bearded man with a hood up. Average and tall build, red beard. He sat a few seats away and listened while the girls talked, simultaneously watching the television screens that showed the games. Later in the arcade, attached, she would see another familiar face of a woman with blonde curly hair that draped past her shoulders.

She dares not allow herself to believe her eyes or even consider the options. As Annie drove to see Marie, she prepared herself to see Chris. What would she do and say? Anastasia took deep breaths and pushed forward instead of running. The reactions he normally garnered from her.

Though she refused to tell Marie, she knew it was Chris. Her subconscious caught on first, and she decided to tell Marie of Dimitri's connections in the government and the service industry. Marie smiled, laughed, and said, "He would know those people." She went on to tell her friend Dimitri that she was on special forces. All things Chris overheard. It seemed they had prepared for this as they spoke of the horrid things he had done in the car outside of the bar arcade before entering.

Annie kept looking over to see the man only face forward with his hood up. Soon they finished their meal and decided to go play arcade games. When Anastasia got up to start, Chris was gone. But as they filtered through the games, Chris's girlfriend kept popping up to see where Anastasia was. Annie kept her mask off to give them all a good, hard look.

No one confronted her. No one spoke with her other than Marie and her friend. The night wound down, and the pop-ups stopped. Then Marie decided it was getting late, seeing the exhaustion on Annie's face, and left to get more food. Anastasia walked as she analyzed her instincts.

Were they true? Did he come to listen to her talk? Did his girlfriend fall into the trap Annie had so many years ago? Falling in love with someone who will always monitor you but never be true and loyal. Much like a tiger in a cage, that is what Anastasia felt like.

Chris would poke her, egg her on, feed her only a little so she stayed hungry, then send her out to do his dirty work. Today she has to pick up the pieces and figure out how much she has done. Why was she so numb to horrible things? Day by day, moment by moment, and prayer by prayer, God would help her understand more, and the things she needed to know would surface.

Quietly, she prayed, almost finished with the perimeter of the yard now, as her head fell. "Please God bless and make a way. Please heal and guide. Thank you, God." A blanket prayer would do for now as her walk came to a close. She still had not sorted out her feelings.

She just knew she was happy to be on this land, with this

husband, in this house, with these kids, and as a child of the one true God through Jesus Christ. She took deep breaths as she entered reality. She could feel the rocks of the driveway under her feet: crunch, crunch, crunch. Feel the wind blowing on her face and the sun kissing the top of her head.

Closing her eyes for a moment. Breathing in the newness and letting go of the old. Out goes the old with her deep breath. Though she still had very shallow breathing, she knew even that could be healed by God. One at a time.

Chapter Fifteen

It was New Year's Day, and Anastasia and Dimitri, along with their three children, were sick from the holiday celebrations and festivities. But the weather was warm again on a New England winter day. The kids went up for a nap as Dimitri and Anastasia wrestled the pine tree they bought for Christmas out the door. The door was neither tall nor wide enough to fit such a specimen. Annie and Dimitri soon realized this fact and ended up dislodging it from its holder and pulling it out of the trunk.

"This way, the branches won't fight us," said Annie. Dimitri considered her option for a few moments, then agreed. Anastasia loved that he did not take everything at face value. In fact, he was quite the rebel, much like her father, Angus. Growing up, Rose and Angus had quite the fun relationship in this area. You see, Rose was a purist, a perfectionist, and everything by the rules.

However, Angus, though it was in his nature to be the same, decided to fight against this fabric. Anastasia found this very entertaining. Rose taught Annie and her siblings to always be safe and know the rules, while Angus taught them where they could bend the rules. Angus never settled for face value and, to this day, refuses to. Anastasia knew she needed that in a husband if she was ever to marry.

Though when she was younger, she thought that looked different. She saw the trait as anarchist and praised it in Chris. But unlike Angus, Chris always took things too far and passed them off as goofy. Annie never liked this. Where Angus would touch a monument until he was warned away, Chris would deface the monument or use it to get a rise out of people in some other way.

Where Angus would egg a bull on with the kids present then make everyone get away before it started charging, Chris would wait to see it charge and hide behind Annie to see what she did. The rebel spirit was much different in them. Then Anastasia met Dimitri. Dimitri was the perfect combination of Rose and Angus in this area. Anastasia found out early on, Dimitri would take extremely calculated risks and at times things at face value.

Anastasia fit perfectly. Where Dimitri refused to take risks, Anastasia would push the line and vice versa. For instance, Dimitri hated it when the kids ate on the couch, but Anastasia simply cleaned up after. Anastasia hated not giving the kids enough attention (though she never knew what that truly meant). Dimitri would make them play with each other and do a practice he called "Strategic Neglect".

Dimitri would stand a room away where the kids could not see him and read his newspaper. This gave the kids the teamwork and confidence Annie could not seem to give them. Then occasionally, he would step in and play with them. Anything they wanted for a period, then back to the other room to listen but not interact. Dimitri and Anastasia had little experience together outside of the home.

But Dimitri's rebellious spirit in the homemade Anastasia rejoice and regularly reflect on her own father's crafted ways of dealing with her and her siblings. When Anastasia was a kid, it was Angus who held her and her siblings loosely and gave them the freedom to learn themselves. Rose was so overwhelmed and scared that they would die or she would do something wrong that she organized most things, even groundings ended in her trying to help and entertain. Angus, instead, would just sit with them or have them go off and play. Though Rose had them play outside a lot or downstairs, it always felt different to Anastasia.

Angus used tactics to entertain like telling jokes or challenging the kids. Once he took the kids to a casino to pull the slot machine. He asked Rose to be the getaway driver. She refused to be an accomplice. He loaded up the machines and had them all pull together as the security zeroed in. Then he told them all to run for the door and try to stay together.

This would go down as one of the most fun experiences Anastasia had as a child. For the simple fact of telling, Rose did get into the driver's seat to pick up the family after they all ran out of the casino and drove off quickly. They laughed harder than they had in a while, as a family unit. Anastasia hoped she and Dimitri would be able to do similar fun things with their kids as they grew. One day at a time.

Chapter Sixteen

Anastasia's body ached from her sickness. She filtered back into the person she was while she was sick. Thoughts run through her head of small mistakes she made in the past that had no effect any more. Though she used them to ground her in the past, now it was natural for her to experience them when she had no energy to fight them off. Thoughts like the time she soloed for her college Christian club and mixed up the notes, then apologized the rest of the way through the song.

Or at that time, she said that one thing to one person, and it was mean. Anything and everything her mind could conjure up would make her feel like a despicable person as she grasped for small, quick breaths. Realizing she now found it too difficult for her to take even one deep breath. Anastasia fought these thoughts by reminding herself they were one of dozens of interactions, and one bad move out of dozens was not horrible, maybe even human. It did not make her a horrible person.

She also prayed fervently and tried to give it to God as much as her subconscious and conscious combined would allow. As she thought and compared horrible things, a date early on with Chris crept into her head. One night in spring, he took her walking through the woods by his house. It was very dark that night, and Chris told Anastasia he wanted her to meet his friend. His friend, who was a homeless man, slept on his and his mom's porch every so often.

Anastasia held Chris's hand and blindly followed

considering such a thing as romantic. Now the trees blocked out the moon, but Chris kept pressing forward and speaking with Anastasia. He drew her deeper and deeper into the wooded lot. She started to feel a weird yearning in her spirit, the words "Do not go left, go right." Of course, Chris wanted to go left "Just ahead," he said.

Anastasia's stomach started to hurt more and more the further they went, and the voice got louder, almost booming now: "DO NOT GO LEFT, GO RIGHT NOW!" Anastasia pulled at Chris and told him there was something bad left. Let's go right. Chris kept going, so Annie let go of his hand and started walking right. He giggled and said, "Okay, let's go right, but let's take the path."

Annie said, "Okay."

Then he got her to a bench still in the woods after he took her on the path right, and she said, "Thank you for coming with me. There was something bad back there. In fact, we should probably get out of the woods now." Chris slowly left Anastasia realizing he came out as a hero again when, in fact, he was trying to kill her. However Annie would reflect years later and realize what was supposed to happen that night.

Another day, he tried to kill her. Chills still ran down her spine as she reflected. "That is a bad person." Chris was not always bad. To Annie, he was the worst when he found he could not kill her.

God spoke to her and protected her the numerous times he tried. He then decided he would turn her into a soulless person and use her as a weapon. Anastasia never even considered someone could do such a thing, especially someone who claimed they loved her. She came out of her memory as she relived the feelings of that night—the sight of the woods around her, the urgings of Chris, and his tugging at her hand. Dimitri had yet to do anything so brazen.

However, he took Anastasia's special skills for granted. This reminded her to vow to never use them unless she were to train her children or she needed to protect her family. She so badly wished she could show him, then maybe he would not question her abilities. She knew that was another lie from the devil and his brood of demons. Those skills were only necessary when it was time—not to flaunt and certainly not to use on those you love.

She left him with the words, "When Chris comes, as he most assuredly will, let me deal with him. He may be a crazy, narcissistic sociopath, but he fears me. He trained me, and in everything, I surpassed him." She would not add that she lacked certain skills, like skills in throwing knives. In fact, that is why Chris haunted her and her family in the shadows.

Not just to try and make them look crazy, which was a tactic. But because he feared what Anastasia would do to him, Anastasia presented itself more powerfully because what is crazier than a sociopathic narcissist? A person who gets knocked down by them then gets up and runs at them over and over, no matter the danger. Anastasia had healed immensely since the last time she spoke with Chris.

She is no longer truly insane, but she never let go of the switch. She would choose the right time to turn her dragon on to finally ward Chris off for good. Her plan was to internally wound him, as there was too much at stake at this point in her life. She needed to make sure he would not get back up and run toward her family, but also that she would not go to prison for what she knew needed to be done. She did consider all the options of torture and marriage.

She knew that would not go well as there were eyes and ears

everywhere. Anastasia realized the memory made her start to panic and go into fight mode. She once again tried to pull out of it. Now taking as deep of a breath as possible. She looked around her and changed her thoughts to the couch she had been lounging on trying to get comfortable.

The little voices upstairs gave her hope and purpose, even in this moment. God gave them to her and Dimitri to steward. Looking up at the family pictures that surrounded her that Dimitri worked so hard to put up on the walls of their gorgeous colonial home out the window, there was a thin dusting of white crystal-like snow white, which represented purity and innocence, much like those babies upstairs.

They did not need the lethal Annie; they just needed a consistent, compassionate, and loving mama. Daddy was the main protector, Anastasia vowed to wait until the time came to show that side of herself. "One more day, I am promised my wildest dreams. A husband who is wonderful and loves me. Three gorgeous, incredible children I did not think I could have.

"Chris may have robbed me of, as much as I was willing to give him, which was everything at that time. But he cannot rob me of this. Only God and I have control over that. What I choose to place my mind on, what I choose to hold onto, and who I choose to contact. He or she no longer has any bearing on my life. Just memories I filter through and pray through to heal.

"The more I work and pray, and the further I get, the better. This is my reality today. Tomorrow is not promised, and today is a present—a miracle I would not have had if I stayed. I would not have had today if my God, the Holy Spirit, Jesus Christ, were not so gracious, merciful, holy, and powerful. If he did not love me and have a plan for me.

"So many times, I was written off in the script of my life to die. But today I rejoice in the fact that I never did die. So many prayers for death, and yet I am still here. I am barely breathing in survival mode most of the time, but I am surrounded by a loving God and His miracles for my life.

"Back then, I was alone, waiting to strike when told, willing to do anything to worship the man I loved instead of my God, who is perfect and loves me back." As the reader, have you ever felt like this? What can you look around at and say, I am blessed; God is real and loves me? What is your miracle?

Rejoice, for today is the present, and your God in heaven loves you. He formed you in your mother's womb, and he walks with you each day. To God, you are His beloved child and co-heir with Christ. Rise above your fears because we only have to fear the creator of all things.

He will protect you until it is time to rejoin Him in heaven, precious child of God. Let Him who has brought you to this point lead you on and be your guide in all things, and one step at a time, we will heal. One day, one breath, one moment—a choice to praise God in our pain instead of giving it space in our everyday lives. Do not give up or give in to the demons trying to rob you of your life.

Chapter Seventeen

Maria was in pain as she rested on the couch beside Anastasia, thrown into a fury of conversation as they had been the night before. They both shared different pieces of their lives' journey while drinking coffee and Annie her energy drink. She could feel her anxiety grow inside her. They laughed and chatted about different worlds that had become theirs. However when Annie attempted to explain why she loved the commander of Dimitri's unit, it set her off the edge.

The commander, who had gone out and done his job when he passionately wanted to protect those he fought for, was held back. This made him insane. He redacted himself from his position and moved back into his parents' basement. During that time, he brought himself back from insanity. As a successful man who was the boss of his unit, had a longstanding girlfriend, and owned his own home, he lived life as a normal human being.

Walking amongst the people who would only see him for the man he presented today. But he knew the dark secrets of a past he wished so heavily to forget. A past that, like most military members came back to haunt him. Some dealt with it in dreams, some with flashbacks, some through substance abuse, and some had been hunted down and killed after the fact. Even some, like Annie's uncle, had the institution they worked for kill them because they knew too much and became a liability instead of an asset.

This had become more and more blatant and common. While

the rest of the world watched movies like "Bourne Identity," these men and women lived them. Those who got higher and higher feared more for their lives from the hands that fed them than any perceived enemy at a given time. Wars were conflicts started by masterminds that hid behind walls and created the illusion of sincere troubles. These were the people who told the masses whom to fight and whom to befriend.

Though it was a strategy for gain and loss as they dictated. One day it was to befriend Native Americans; the next it was "they are the enemy, kill." The French, the Germans, the Russians—even your own brothers—from a different mindset. As the civil war was created based on the divide between good slave owners' and bad ones. All owning servants of the field and home.

Same as today, those same people are pushing the divide between sex, races, and religions: "except everyone, but make sure you know you are bad for this".

"Hate cops because they are evil and kill instead of protecting. Put cameras up everywhere so you are safer; make sure you go green because it gives you more freedom." Though that means they can shut you down anytime they want, and is green cheaper? Anastasia wrestled with ideas as she processed what the commander and so many others who were faithful servants had done throughout the course of history.

She recalled even soldiers in concentration and extermination camps being forced to: 1) work for the cause. 2) not be nice, or they and their families would be killed. 3) See and embrace the plan for one man who did not set foot on the soil of either concentration camp or an extermination camp. Many would see such warriors throughout history and wonder, How could they kill? Then, if asked if it were you or the other guy, what would you do?

Only to answer, I would come out alive. Was this a truce? At war, when your leader is commanding you to live or die for the cause, you are to do what you feel best. Even Russians, when they fought, would either kill or, if they retreated, be killed by their leaders. This became a common thing during their wars.

So, they refused to back down because, no matter their course, they would die. As well, the enemy was much easier to take on than the people who knew everything about them and their families. This was the rule for warriors: love nothing, and if you do, don't share that love with anyone. Why is it a rule? Because it gives others power.

The first step to destroying a singular person is to use what you love and feel connected to against you. If that did not work, it gave those people less power. After childhood, Anastasia feigned importance for things she no longer cared about. This importance made people feel connected to her and share their stories. However, when the evil people tried to pull the plug, and many did try, they were surprised to see very little reaction out of an extremely adamant Annie who promised she cared for such things.

This was not a lie. At one time, she did care for all those items listed. Now detached from those feelings, she refused to let them overtake her. That was the game of a warrior. Rose and Angus were excellent at teaching the kids to be warriors and why they needed such skills.

Anastasia came back to the room and heard herself speaking to Marie. Now it was about Albert's first Easter. She came upstairs to be yelled at by Phillip, who was in a rage about finding his sheets messed up and Chris's bracelet on the bed. As he yelled, he was astonished.

1) He did not know it was Chris. 2) It was somehow her fault. 3) Albert started his first Easter with this toxicity. Annie took a deep breath and started to explain. When Phillip heard her explanation, he accepted the fact that it did not play into his fear of adultery by him or his wife. Moments later, Phillip acted as though everything was all right.

Annie started to attempt to calm her panic attack and get back on track to make Easter a good day for Albert. It took hours before she felt good again. She found herself yelling at Marie while she stared into her eyes. "Why would you expect anything less? Oh, you felt affronted.

"Why? Because someone was in your space? Because someone had the audacity to leave an item behind? Yet you are partnering with that same someone to let the crazy touch an infant. That same someone would rather see that infant dead or severely damaged than alive and thriving.

"That same someone who your sister is fighting for her life from. Yet he makes one wrong move in your book, and that's it. Now it's my fault, and I need to deal with both sides." Marie stayed calm and changed the subject as Annie felt her rage and attempted to locate the epicenter and breathe it out. Soon they silenced, and when Anastasia was fully back and present, she apologized.

To which Marie replied, "It's okay. But I won't continue that path or meet your aggression. If I feel aggrieved at whether you meant it or not. What I will do is let you vent, rage vent even, until I am over stimulated by it, then change the subject or walk away." Annie appreciated her honesty and felt her heart swell inside her.

She reminded herself and Marie that this was the correct course and the healthiest option. She also vowed to release a memory from years prior. This specific memory, knowing it no longer was her life. Now she was a mom of three and a wife to one incredible man. With Dimitri, her title felt more like queen than what it would have felt like with Chris.

With Chris, the title of leading lady had only one name: slave. She would have been a slave to Chris. Marriage felt like the gift of a life with a best friend she never knew would come; hers was Dimitri. Instead of a funeral, that was the start of a million deaths. With Chris, Anastasia felt like every day was an opportunity for him to kill off another part of her beautiful nature and get inside her head.

He took it as an everyday challenge. Dimitri fought for the opposite. His dream was to renew and rebirth the woman she was and the pieces she had lost. To allow God to bring forth the truest parts of Anastasia and for her to use those parts daily to live her fullest life. Anastasia attempted such love for Dimitri as well.

God was a main force in their love and life, from parenting to work to interactions with loved ones, all the way down to their own personal relationships. They both avidly sought the creator of all and prayed for his infinite will and wisdom. They gave themselves and all they had back to God to be used daily. This was the love Anastasia needed and had been missing. Though they were imperfect and hurt each other from time to time, their relationship did not solely rely on such small details.

They were loved perfectly by God and imperfectly by each other, and the combination made for healing and life to blossom forth between the cracks. There was no doubt they were in God's hands, and he healed their minds and hearts. No doubt their kids would be richly blessed and gifted, as Dimitri and Anastasia had all their lives. With a divine connection to the life-giver, counselor, healer, Alpha and Omega, God of Gods, Lord of Lords. This changed the course of their lives, and fighting through life together with the same faith made each moment feel like a blessing and each gift like a miracle.

They made their purposes grow like trees that had deep roots pointing up toward their Father in Heaven and branches that extended down and out to the ones they loved. While they broke off leaves and flowers and dropped fruits for their community, God gave them more to grow and give. This was the life of any Christ follower. When the roots withered and turned down toward the world, so would the tree. But when they pointed up toward God, the tree blossomed eternally.

Anastasia, Dimitri, Albert, Rosie, and Scott all devoted their energy to rooting in God and letting him discern what leaf, flower, fruit, or branch should be where. Through faith, God would guide them and without faith, they would become blind to their purpose. Making them fail to glorify God at the time brought forth the same reason Abraham could not go to the Promised Land. He had lost faith and plummeted into fear and his own strength. However he was a great leader with God.

He lacked God. David lost his kingship many times and wandered like a homeless vagabond because of his lack of faith. Though he had God's heart (because he did not seek to sin but to glorify God), he was richly blessed when devoted to God. He also had times of sin and clung to fear. Paul was a man of faith but faced much persecution because of his lack of faith at the beginning of his life. Judas had been a follower of Christ and spent most of his days in faith.

But when he turned to clinging to fear instead, he went down in history as the man who turned Jesus into the one to be crucified. After he realized what he had done, it was his fear and sin that pushed him to kill himself. Many men and women throughout history lost faith and clung to fear and sin. Anastasia prayed God would help them no longer live that life and raise their kids to be children of God and strong in their faith, as Rose and Angus had taught their kids.

Chapter Eighteen

It was not long after Anastasia suggested that Dimitri had a provocative dream. In fact, she had a dream about Michael Jordan (a famous basketball player from the 1990s) that she would consider a "provocative dream". When she woke up, she confessed her human tendency to Dimitri and apologized. To which Dimitri responded, "At least it was Michael Jordan." Anastasia felt relieved, but she had a feeling in her heart and mind.

She recalled dreams and moments like this in the past. To be honest, she and Chris had a rather progressive sexual life. Chris told Anastasia he liked to wake up to her playing with his sexual organs. Anastasia would do that to please him. But when Chris played with Annie while she slept, she did not wake up.

She would just have livid dreams and wake up feeling off. Chris really liked doing this to her. He would wait until she was sleeping and do what he wanted, only for her to wake up, not knowing what happened. She recalled many mornings waking up and feeling that disgusting feeling inside, knowing he had taken advantage of her and yet saying nothing about it. Even when Albert was an infant, she had these experiences.

At that time, Chris had been breaking into her parents' house, where she stayed. But likely the most prominent consideration that allowed her the idea that these were not just disgusting dreams that her subconscious put together. Always being fooled around when she did not want it. Anastasia did not recall how Albert was made. She regularly looked back at the day falling thoughts and feelings, bringing her mind back to it all.

It was after Christmas, only a few days. She was on a mission to end it with her current boyfriend, but she knew the only way she would let herself off the hook from his demands. The demands of an open relationship with a man who wanted to act faithful and act as if they would marry but did not want to be faithful. Getting sexual favors elsewhere during the short few months they knew each other. The only way to match evil was to cheat.

Anastasia held herself to an extremely high standard, even though she knew what it was and that most of the current population would not consider it cheating. She called it that to release herself from the family get-togethers and bar times she had allowed him to drag her to. In fact, they had quite a rocky relationship, and it had likely been open from the start. Her later finding out that the girl he called sister that Annie pried about was his wife. Anastasia was devastated to be the woman he cheated with.

So she cheated on him. She got Chris and herself drunk and forced him to take her home with him. Chris was a pushover, ironically, when it came to Annie. If she asked what he wanted her to do, he would go with it and let her think it was her idea. She took him home, and instead of sleeping together, he used one of her body parts to orgasm, then she separately orgasmed while he was in the bathroom.

The next morning, she woke up and called her soon-to-be ex-open relationship boyfriend, claiming she did something horrible. To Anastasia, it was and felt horrible. Her last resort. To her soon-to-be ex, he was mad but knew he had no ground to stand on as Annie had been loyal while he had not. Not just his wife but other women in the area he had been with during their few short months.

The call ended with a breakup, and Chris was happy to see

Annie in the morning. Annie had become one of those girls who left before falling asleep. But she needed support to do what she had to to get out of the weird relationship she was in. Who better than the guy who was obsessed with her and refused to allow her to be with any other guy? If he found out she was dating, he would do whatever she could to break them up, even if he was in another relationship, because in his mind, he owned her.

Anastasia still questioned how and what happened. How could she have gotten Albert out of such a situation? But she was grateful for Albert. Even thinking about that period in her life made her feel disgusted inside and cringe at the thought of how low her abusive relationship brought her. Out of ashes, God brings beauty.

Out of the ashes of those years in and out of what most would call a deadly relationship came Albert. In turn, Dimitri fell in love with the scorned and very serious Anastasia. Then, through Dimitri, Anastasia was gifted with Rosie and Scott. Four beautiful miracles occurred after she thought her life was over. Now she sits and stares at those miracles while they lay on the living room floor, playing.

Dimitri is on the bottom, giggling and taking blows from Rosie and Albert as they climb all over "Daddy!" Scott is sitting in the walker made of plastic and cloth, smiling as he watches the action, his eyes bright and wide, most assuredly eager to do such things when he is a little older. Anastasia is sitting on the couch overlooking the living room with a devilish smile and a giggle occasionally as she rejoices over God's precious gifts. Soon to break up the attack on Dimitri because he refuses to do it himself. As he soaks up the painful hugs and kisses, he knows he only has a limited number of years to get.

Chapter Nineteen

It was one of those days where Anastasia sat and thought of all the things she had done wrong within the last few weeks. Considering how Dimitri had bested her in too many things. Trying to fight the sickness that plagued her body, but somehow letting the sickness take over her mind. She knew she should walk the land and ground it back into what God had given her. Instead, she turned to her phone (an iPhone) and television to solve her thoughts.

The only problem was that they only ramped up her fears. Making her believe she and her beloved had more trials than they truly did. Just yesterday, she felt such relief throwing away mugs from the past she had held onto for others, thinking they would come back to collect. But they never did. Life moved on, and with that, so did her friends.

Annie was the youngest of five, and her bedroom was at the end of the long hallway in a country ranch house. Because of this, people defaulted on throwing any extra items they did not want Rose to find upon coming home into Anastasia's room. Rose was notorious for getting extremely angry if the house was "a mess" when she got home. It took a little while for her kids to understand what "a mess" meant. But soon they realized it meant items sitting out in the living room and kitchen, especially stuff on the ground.

So, they would scramble when Rose got home to avoid the yelling and pick up as fast as they could. Most of the "pick up" resulted in a pile in Anastasia's room for her to sort later and designate what goes where. *It is funny,* she thought. *I have spent my whole life sorting other people's messes: mental, emotional, and physical messes.* But when it came to mental and emotional messes, Annie became paralyzed if she had to deal with her own. Other people she could help, but only prayer helped her.

Anastasia was not bitter about the agreed-upon solution back in those days and found she was not always the one sent to sort the pile. No, they all worked to avoid the stern Rose in the areas they could figure out. Rose was stern but very kind. When the kids abided by her rules, she was the most loving and caring woman. But she lacked boundaries, and when the kids tried to figure out lines not to cross, Rose rarely afforded options.

In fact, Anastasia could explain it as searching for land mines. Rose was pleasant as you walked through her mine field until you took the wrong turn, and BOOM! Rose was yelling and screaming, and the kids were left to find the remains and retrace their steps to what led up to the mine. So Rose did not blow up another time in that area. Anastasia realized after years that much of what happened was because Rose was without community and had very few breaks. If she fixed something, it took time and energy, and the kids cared very little, then boom.

She had very little energy, very little time, and very little space and she lived what Annie would call an overworked, overwhelmed life. Rose would have to forcefully take time away because her purist self would only allow guilt in regard to getting what she needed for her family. Like most women, if Rose had allowed herself less guilt and more freedom, she would have had more fun in this stage of life. Instead of land mines for the kids, it could have been more like capturing the flag. Instead of yelling to confirm there was an inconsistency, Rose would find herself laughing off the stupidity of her children doing things that made them kids.

Anastasia played that through her head on many occasions

as she felt herself slip into land mine Rose. Annie fought for more time away when she felt her life feeling more overwhelming and herself becoming too stressed. Anastasia had yet to sleep through a whole night since before Scott was born, and her sanity was hanging on by a thread most days. Dimitri repeated that they should not have more kids yet, or he would go insane and not be able to take it. However, Anastasia knew he said that mostly for her.

She had spent the past few months under the immense stress of the holidays, letting Dimitri know she was miserable and in need of change. They both wanted more kids, but now certainly was not the time. They spent most days regretting moving too fast. Loving their kids with all they had but always working out of a place of emptiness from life, not stopping. With Scott, everything went wrong. He was as fit as a fiddle.

But from day one, they were kept in the hospital longer. Then their parents decided it would be "pleasant" to stay for a visit as they dropped the other kids off. Then everyone wanted to meet and keep seeing Scott repeatedly. Anastasia and Dimitri had no more strength or ability to fight it. This caused them to almost lose everything when Scott was roughly six months old.

They had been pushed to their limits, and their families and friends kept pushing, not understanding what they were doing. Anastasia and Dimitri kept placating everyone. It still ate Anastasia up inside. She loved Dimitri and never thought she would find such a man. A man who put silence and defense to her thoughts of all men.

Even when she tried him in her head with her thoughts, he had shown he did not fit with the bad people but with the good. But even those you love who love you creep in and fester like diseases if you let them. "Anything can creep between you and those you love if you let it and don't fight for the specific things you want. You must always pray for things of the heart and those you love, and never stop fighting. Evil comes in with good intentions at times, and if you cannot smack it down, then you will lose all you have ever wanted and more. Satan and his demons are at work constantly. Do not forget it."

Anastasia listened to the uplifting caution speech from a radio in the distance as she sat at the coffee shop. She loved coffee shops. The ambiance and aroma always made her feel at peace.

She looked down at the picture of Dimitri with the kids on her phone, and her heart sank. One step further and that would never have come. That picture shows their marriage. It is so easy to get wrapped up in the small, fickle things and forget or devalue the giant, important things. Anastasia texted Dimitri, "Thank you for sticking with me. I do not deserve you, but I will continue to love and fight for you as long as we both live."

Dimitri had heard that multiple times, and he was not the wishy-washy one. Anastasia was always more afraid of love and all that coincided than really anything else in the world. Love, marriage, and motherhood hands down proved to be the hardest things Anastasia had ever done. Every day, I wake up to serve, get overwhelmed, be touched, and be needed and followed through the house. Then, when Dimitri came home, he also needed her, and she needed him and time with him, but it all felt so impossible. Anastasia realized her plans and boundaries were being infringed on again and vowed to reestablish them.

For friends and family, it would never be enough. But they're not enough; its already Dimitri and Annie's too much, breaking point. Angus and Rose understood, had respect, and found perks in keeping space. But it was time to keep the once-a-month promise with the other grandparents, and those who wanted to see them could fit into those times. Because although Annie was a stay-at-home mom, "They have so much time, right?"

She certainly has less time now than ever before in her life. It made her consider how she had made moms feel in the past or present. Anastasia certainly was a very selfish being who lacked much wisdom and knowledge, and many times even her best intentions came out as bad. People tended to keep her at arm's length at this point in life. For which she could not blame them.

She knew some things she had done and was slowly filtering through the things she did that she blocked. Taking moments that were certainly not hers to have and not letting people have them to mourn their losses. Making those moments about herself, in turn, made her a failure in many things. She knew she was human and had to face herself at the end of the day.

Therefore, she needed to be kind and forgive herself for that moments she held onto those others, had already forgotten. "We must forgive our pasts so we can forgive others and when we release one piece, a new piece of the puzzle of life will be revealed to us." Recovery is one step at a time. Some people were not as lucky as Anastasia, locked in a house with three little ankle biters and her thoughts for ten-plus hours a day.

Clearly, God designed time to heal and release her past so she could move onto her future. Motherhood looked very different in Anastasia's day, there was no such thing as community. If she did not have God, she would have gone insane long ago. "Be grateful for this opportunity completely given by God and try to make the best out of each day" is Anastasia's mantra.

Chapter Twenty

Dimitri stood by Anastasia faithfully as she fought the sickness that seemed never-ending. Anastasia was extremely grumpy and ready for a fight when she was sick. Many people could not stand her even more than on a regular basis. Though Annie was very innocent and, at times, ignorant, she was also mean when she was sick. Her body jumped into fight or flight, and she always wanted to fight when she felt weakest.

She also found herself replaying the bad or stupid things she said to those around her. How insensitive and stupid I am, she thought as she worked in the kitchen, preparing an easy breakfast for herself and her family. Anastasia had not yet mastered the general breakfast that she cooks, and everyone just sits and eats. At a time like this, really anything goes for what the kids ask to eat and what she goes for. Serving the kids their hot dogs and ketchup for breakfast, her husband his bagel with cream cheese and iced coffee (he did not ask for it) and herself a slice of bread toasted to a crisp stacked with cream cheese and blueberries.

I was completely forgetting about the baby until Dimitri chimed in. He came to the kitchen and heated up some butternut squash that was reserved in the fridge for their little one, who had yet to pop any teeth. Scott took bites pleasantly but found it hard to breathe while working through the mash, so he started eating slower. Albert shoved his hotdog into his mouth, overly excited that he could eat it for breakfast. Then, in a flash, I was in the kitchen, head hovering over the trashcan, retching the hot dog out.

It took a few moments before Anastasia realized what was going on. But when she did, she patted his back and tried to comfort him. Then asked what had happened, "I shoved too much in my mouth," stated Albert. Anastasia understood this only happened because Albert was also struggling to breathe that morning. Anastasia gave each child and herself a puff of an old inhaler she had lying around from Albert's last asthma attack.

True to form, Rosie picked at her food. It was only a few months ago that she would eat every bite in one sitting. But now she only picked at whatever food was set in front of her and rarely finished even her favorite dishes. Dimitri finished feeding Scott, and then quickly ate what Anastasia had placed in front of him. Anastasia was onto the next meal request before she had a chance to eat her breakfast.

"Booberries, pate," Rosie stated as she pointed to her plate. Annie gently placed blueberries on Rosie's plate.

"Cheesy rice," Albert called in from the living room while he sat and watched cartoons. He is now fully recovered from throwing up and relaxing his body while hydrating. Normally, Anastasia would not allow such disrespect, but she had no energy to fight it.

She came with warm, cheesy rice. She was able to eat her toast and sip her coffee moments later. Rosie was begging for bites of Annie's toast. Rosie loved to share people's food with them and her food with others.

Many days she would call everyone to the table at mealtime and say, "Don't eat! Niko eat!" This loosely translated to: "Jonny, come and eat! Niko, it is time to eat!" Annie called Rosie her Greek mama, always wanting to take care of people, and of utmost importance was making sure people ate and ate so much they were ready to pop.

Anastasia grew up in a home where she was required to finish the plate Rose put together. These plates usually held a portion size for two adults, not just one, and certainly not a fully grown woman's portion. As many know, a healthy adult woman must have smaller portions to stay skinny as their metabolism slows while as they age. To Dimitri's mom, no one could eat enough. If you ate a small portion in her house, she saw it as an immense insult.

She made delicious food, and Annie regularly found herself eating far too much and then licking the plate clean before she was done. In turn, being called a pig in Greek, when she could not get enough and ate off her kids plates, she knew they would not finish. Annie was used to Irish-English meals that she loved, as Angus and Rose were great cooks. But the Greek-Mediterranean food tasted like a slice of heaven due to how new and healthy it was. She knew it would be a good life learning to cook this and eating the food her mother-in-law and husband made.

Part Two

Chapter One

It was Dimitri's birthday, but the family was still sick, and Annie was never one for parties. So instead, she prayed that God would give her something creative and fun to do for him. One big piece was not to control him; let him do what he wanted to do. The second piece was to try to make a game out of finding his well-thought-out gifts. She only got him two this year.

Both of which Annie really put her heart into. Still, it can seem sad to only open a few gifts as an adult when you spend your childhood being showered with them. She pulled Albert, Rosie, and Scott to the side and asked them to help her. They would make a special gift edition scavenger hunt for dad's birthday. Rosie just wanted "my daddy" and Scott just wanted mommy "Wahh".

But Albert was extremely excited. He immediately started looking for places they could hide the gifts for "Daddy's birthday". They scoured the house to see what places would be most effective. Would the dining room, which held a table and two bookshelves, work to hide one of the small gifts? Maybe the mudroom with its bench and shoe rack.

Or even the kitchen, which held cabinets galore to torture Dimitri into looking through each one before he could find his gift. Soon they decided it was best to hide both gifts in the living room. This room held the most promise for low hiding spots. Spots that could be reached with little hands while aiding in making this fun game for Daddy. They chose the blanket bin and the magazine bin as the perfect places for the necklaces Annie got.

One necklace was to represent their fated partnership. It held a jade pendant that had a dragon and phoenix on it. The other necklace was a trinket to remind Dimitri how precious he was to God and his family. It was a cross that had the picture of his saint in the center. Once they found where to hide the gifts, they started to make clues for their scavenger hunt.

"The sun rises in the east and sets in the west. Your first clue is on the north side of the house."

Another clue read, "This is what I, Annie, wish for our home. A single word that encompasses so many meanings." Dimitri finished his required work and got up to figure out the breakdown of each clue.

Though he had four assistants if he needed them, two are very eager to be in Daddy's company, one looking to be held and carried through the hunt, and the last is a loving wife with good intentions. They all slowly moved around the house as a sort of blob of love. Dimitri entered a room, as did his entourage. He exited a room, and the family followed.

Anastasia giggled as she watched the show from the rear of the group. Each person was so enthralled by the event itself, though it lasted only a few minutes. As the game ended, everyone settled back into the living room, and Dimitri opened his gifts. He made some jokes about them as he fought back tears. Anastasia, feeling the emotion, decided it would be fun to gather everyone's pendants and take a picture of them all.

Her mind went directly to where she had stowed each member of her family's pendants. Mostly in baby boxes. Only to find she had not gotten one for sweet Rosie, or hers was lost in the moves. So instead, she came back downstairs defeated and got online to order her pendant for a future picture. Dimitri was still beaming as Annie explained, and he stated, "It is all right, my love. Thank you for these beloved presents. I can tell they are from your heart, and I love them." With a kiss on her forehead and then a gentle hug. A pendant at birth was a Chinese tradition. Those would be animals chosen by the parents that would help guide each child throughout their lives.

Sometimes they would become them, and sometimes those animals would balance out their weaknesses. But they would never leave them alone. For Albert, Annie chose a tiger. Though she had struggled to decide between wolf and tiger, finally she landed on tiger because that was most like her, and she knew Albert would be very similar. Rosie Annie chose an owl.

The owl was the goddess Athena's animal and represented wisdom. The owl was also known as the tiger of the air. For Scott, Annie was also confused for a time. She chose to give him the bee. The bee was steady and hardworking.

They never complained, and when it came to fighting, they would always get their stinger in. Anastasia also had the most bee attention while pregnant with Scott, which ultimately made her decide on that animal. Though early on, Scott was a survivor and steady. He knew what he wanted and how to get it. He certainly had the persistence of a bee.

Soon after the scavenger hunt, the kids were sent to naptime. Anastasia and Dimitri were able to go over why the presents were chosen and what they represented. Dimitri beamed and let Annie take pictures of him. Then they held each other in a long embrace, which they both desperately needed. Naptime felt like it flew by that day, and then it was ice cream cake-making time.

The kids suited up by rolling their sleeves and each getting a spoon. Annie pulled out the cookies, which would reside in the middle of the cake. They were gluten-free Oreos. Then came the beloved chocolate and vanilla ice cream. The kids cheered as the ice cream hit the table and all lifted their spoons.

Annie reminded them they could have bites, but most of it needed to go in the cake. They nodded their heads in agreement. "Okay, you guys scoop the chocolate ice cream into the cake pan first while I put the cookies in the bag to be smashed." The kids gladly pulled the ice cream carton to them while Scott squealed in excitement, knowing he would soon have a taste. Annie filled the bag and brought out the meat tenderizer mallet.

Albert was excited to try it. After a few hits, she took over, knowing that all the cookie pieces would go flying if she let him continue. It was not long before the cookies went on, then the vanilla layer, and back into the freezer until after dinner. The kids sat at the counter as Annie started to pull together Dimitri's favorite dish, Shepherd's Pie. A family recipe passed down from Rose.

After she peeled and chopped the potatoes, she threw them in a pot with chopped garlic and onions. By that time, the kids were bored with cooking and baking and realized they would not get any more ice cream. Off they went back into the playroom and let Annie have the space she needed to move forward in her cooking journey. The night was filled with laughter, good food, and love as it came to a close with dinner and a movie. Thirty-seven did not look so bad after all to Dimitri.

Chapter Two

It was a cold winter day as Anastasia, Dimitri, and the kids suited up to go play outside at the kid's request. Annie reveled in taking the kids out. Though it was always a challenge to get three tiny kids all weather-ready and out, she decided to make the two older children help. They got all their gear on with a little help from Anastasia and Dimitri. Then Scott was suited up, and they went out the backdoor.

As Annie was outside and the snow was falling around her and her little family, she thought of all the times she had gone out in the snow just like this with Chris. Chris was a snowplow guy by trade. He would wait until the storms passed, then wake up and plow driveways all night so customers could get out of their driveways in the morning. Sometimes he allowed Anastasia to join him. She loved going with him on his snowplowing run.

As they drove, they would pull people out of ditches, and when they were hungry, they would stop at the gas station to fuel up with gas and food. This was, by far, one of Anastasia's favorite times with Chris. Butterflies fluttered through her stomach, thinking about it and wondering if Dimitri would do the same type of work when he retired from the military. While they drove around, people would come running out, asking them to plow their driveways for cash. Chris would always take them up on it to get cash in his pocket.

Anastasia only went three times with him. The last time she ventured out with Chris was a day much like today. Chris and

Anastasia were fighting, like always. She forced him to let her go snowplow with him. He slept until three a.m. so he could work through the morning.

But of course, Chris could not make it easy on Anastasia. He kept the plans vague because he did not want her to come with him. Anastasia was stubborn. She spent that evening in the town he would work in. She drove around, helping people out.

First, she drove two people walking in the snow to their dorm after failing to get their van unstuck from the snow it had slid into. Then she pushed out a white Mustang with a Chinese man in it. He offered her dinner, but she refused by saying she had friends waiting for her in the car. Instead, she drove around looking for anyone else stupid enough to get out in the storm. Soon Chris texted, twenty minutes before he told her to meet, with the meeting spot, and ushered her to hurry.

Anastasia excitedly rushed to the meeting spot. She parked her car and walked up to the truck. Chris had the truck locked at first, so Anastasia could not enter. Then he joked as he always did; he tried to drive off without her. But he stopped laughing as he unlocked the doors.

She got into the car as he yelled at her for being late, and how could she not know where to meet him and how three a.m. really meant two forty-five a.m.? Then went on to let her know how she was the problem that would make him late to pick up the giant parking lot he needed to help with. Anastasia stayed quiet and was just happy to be in the car. Chris attacked her more and asked her to get out. Annie sat there.

"Okay, let's go!" They were off to be the unsung heroes of the town again. Chris was pleasant with his regular digs.

"What are you wearing? Could have worn something more appropriate."

"You look so tired and disheveled; why would any guy, especially me, want to show you off? You should make sure no one sees me with you, so I do not look bad."

"Stay quiet while I drive because I do not want your annoying voice distracting me." And so on. Annie and Dimitri saw similar traits in Albert from time to time.

Anastasia attempted to blind herself to them. Dimitri took them on full steam. On that particular day, Albert felt he was not getting enough attention, so he decided to sit in the middle of the floor. Dimitri woke toward him in hopes he would move but realized he would not. "Stupid Albert!" Dimitri exclaimed.

Annie, wishing to protect Albert and not knowing the situation, stated, "Stupid Dimitri! You walked toward him!" Dimitri looked at her, and they spoke about what they saw happen. He told her that Albert was sitting in the middle of the doorway that went from the playroom to the rest of the west side of the house. He spoke about how he asked Albert to move, and he refused, so the next best thing was to step over him.

Which Albert lifted his body at that exact moment just to get hit. Anastasia turned to Albert and asked if it was true. He said, "Yes." Anastasia apologized and faded back into her memory. She finished the driveways and roads with Chris.

He was glad it was over and happily dropped her back at her car before finishing off the last few driveways. Instead of the past, he would finish with her and then they would go eat, he refused to cater to her any more. She still held out hope for their relationship at that time, but Chris refused to give Annie anything good. Even marring the good things and moments with the bad.

Trickling back into reality, the show stopped, and Anastasia was taking Rosie and Albert for a sled ride up the hill of the farm. The hill where she pulled them was steep enough to get her heart racing. Rosie and Albert just sat and embraced the beauty as she pulled and tugged back down the hill. She let the sled go at times for them to really slide. Back at the house, Rosie asked to go in, while Albert asked to stay out.

Dimitri was already inside with Scott. Rosie stepped inside to meet Dimitri, ready to get out of her snow clothes. Back out, Anastasia and Albert decided to clear off the porches around their lovely New England colonial. Albert, after watching Annie do the first porch, decided he would take on the second porch. He shoveled in a different manner than Anastasia, less efficiently.

But she enjoyed every moment of watching him do it. A true farm boy needed to be able to do hard work and know how to do it the best way for himself. She leaned back in the snow and gave him tips and encouragement while he worked. Soon it was time to go inside, much to Albert's dismay. But with his cold, wet hands, there were few options.

Up the stairs, they went into the house, where Dad waited again to strip Albert of his cold, wet winter clothes. Anastasia felt warm and cozy inside as she watched Dimitri take such good care of Albert. Those moments felt like a miraculous dream, and she prayed for more. Often, when they were away from Anastasia, they shared this sweet relationship. While Annie was around and saw their true love for each other, she counted it as a treasure.

Anastasia rejoiced in the love God had given their family for each other. Days like these are few and far between for most parents and children in society today. Many people had to work most days, and their kids were in school or under someone else's watchful eye. Annie knew this was one of the greatest gifts God could give her. She soaked up the moments; she was not trapped in memories from the past, and she hoped one day she would be able to be present in all those special moments.

Chapter Three

Today is Rosie's second father-daughter and mother-daughter special day. Rosie is very young and mostly likes to help around the house, but she also loves books and is very girly. Dimitri decided to take her out first. He started by taking her to the hardware store to get something for the farm. Then I decided to take her to a bookstore called Barnes and Noble.

Dimitri walked with Rosie as she explored the world of books that surrounded her. With eyes lit up and a huge smile, she seemed to be right at home. Much like Rose, who was a librarian, Rosie found solace and purpose in books. Dimitri felt very similar about books, as they helped him learn English after starting school only speaking Greek. English was not spoken in his home as both his parents were Spartans who moved to America. He was the first of three children to start school and was determined to not have his siblings go through the same painful experiences he had been through.

Where teachers and his fellow students could not understand him. Dimitri only found reading to truly help him, so he became a vigorous reader. Grabbing any book he could get his hands on as Rosie meandered through the bookstore, Dimitri realized this was a gift and a bond shared through generations. He smiled. He felt a warmth inside that he never truly considered viable before having a family.

Dimitri always fought to take care of others, as did Anastasia. Even to the point of finding himself the animal whisperer in past relationships. However, nothing compared to staring at his mini-me, Rosie, enjoying the things that he enjoyed. He came back down from cloud nine without losing his warm feelings. Dimitri spoke to Rosie, "What toy would you like, my love?"

Rosie smiled wider and started pointing and touching all the ones she liked. "We must narrow it down to one, Rosie." The search and decision process continued until she found the perfect pair, a book, and a stuffed bunny set. Rosie was satisfied by her choice, and Dimitri was all too ready to purchase the toy book set for his precious daughter. They stood in line, purchased the item, and received a coupon for the café.

Buy one, get one free cookie. Dimitri looked down at the coupon, then to Rosie, then to the café, and thought, *Why not?* They slowly walked to the café as Rosie examined her toy more. Dimitri ordered them two cookies, one apple juice, and one coffee. Then they went and sat at a table.

When they sat down, he broke the first cookie apart, opened her juice, and took a sip of it. "Tax," he said as he swallowed his sip. Dimitri was determined to teach the kids about taxes, which were prevalent in their New England town. It was a fun creative way, as Rosie would spill overfilled juice and see how life worked here. You work, and the first cut of your pay goes to taxes before you can even touch the rest.

Rosie giggled and did not mind one bit. She was so excited to be sitting across from Daddy. Just her and Daddy. She started to tell him all about life in a newly formulated baby babble, which to her sounded completely logical but to Dimitri sounded like noises pushed together. He nodded, smiled, and followed as she told him her thoughts.

She felt extremely loved to be heard and understood by her

very own dad. Such a special bond they had. Soon their drinks and cookies were done, and it was time to head home and rejoin the family. Dimitri would remember this time fondly and continue this course to show Rosie how a man should treat her. He would treasure each date, dance, and event he was able to attend now and in the future.

Gifts he was sure were never to come as he approached 35 with no wife and kids. Now, at 37 he found his mind scrambling as he fought to support and protect three kids and a wife. It seemed like a lifetime alone, and in the blink of an eye, he had all he ever wanted. Now to keep that through hard work, open ears, and lots and lots of prayer. Nothing was promised, but he would enjoy every moment he was given.

Rosie and Anastasia had no idea what they would do for their own date, so they decided to go to the store and get a toy for Scott. Rosie hopped in the car excitedly and said, "Cot present." Anastasia drove them to the store, talking with Rosie. She understood most of what Rosie was trying to say and encouraged her to go on and practice more. Rosie chatted away.

Soon they were at the store. They got out of the car. Anastasia got out first, then opened Rosie's door to find her in her car seat. She unclipped her seatbelt and ushered Rosie into her arms. Rosie loved to be carried by Dimitri and Anastasia.

She embraced the moment as Anastasia moved quickly through the parking lot and into the store. Now in the store, she placed Rosie in a cart, as she needed to get diapers. First, they played race car on the way to the diapers. Rosie giggled as Annie impersonated the voiceover of races. This was a common game to play for Annie while the kids were in the cart.

To the diapers, they raced. Trying to move quickly, Anastasia started talking to Rosie about what sizes they would need. Rosie was in the course of potty training but certainly would not be truly ready to be without diapers for a few more months. Scott needed all the diapers they could afford. They scoured the aisle for exactly what they would need.

Annie tried to stay present but flashed back to her first real job outside of college. She worked in an assisted living home as a residential care aid. Annie loved aspects of the job but hated others. She hated showers but loved spending time with people throughout her shift. She did not mind the diaper changing or toileting most of the time.

But there was one lady she did not like at all. The lady was deaf, and if you made her angry by any stretch, she would smear poop on you while you were putting her next diaper on (as she sat on the toilet). Thankfully, she never did that to Annie. However, she did throw a metal trashcan at her head. Annie slammed the door behind her, and the trashcan thudded into it.

Mostly, diapers meant ripping the sides off and then standing there to place them on patients whose legs were ready as they sat on the toilet. Once on, the patient could stand and then either wipe themselves or Annie would wipe them. Years later, while she was pregnant with Rosie, Annie worked in similar facilities, but not with the geriatric population. She now worked with the clinically insane, mentally and physically handicapped. A memory flashed through her mind.

She kneeled in front of a patient, trying to give him a diaper before bed. In the spirit of efficiency, she did this while he sat on the toilet. She must have made him angry in some way (he was non-verbal), and he came after her. Clawed her down her chest and arms, ripping the skin. Annie felt a connection with this patient and was disappointed that he lashed out at her in this manner. Confused as to why he did this, she looked at him, distancing herself, and asked why he did this.

He started to rock back and forth and move his arms back toward his core. Looking away from her and humming. Anastasia took her cue. "Okay, I will have someone else come put you to bed." Coming back to reality, she and Rosie were standing in the diaper section of the store.

Annie grabbed the diapers she thought best and pushed the cart toward the toys. Rosie touched any toy she could get her hands on. She was excited to get a "cot" (Scott) a toy. They went down the aisle specific to his age range and chose a good toy for her little brother. Then Rosie saw a girly toy that she had to have.

As it was Annie and Rosie's special time, Annie purchased this toy for Rosie. On the way to the register, they picked up some candy to enjoy before returning to the boys. Rosie helped unload the cart at check-out. Off they went back to the car and were on their way to the boys. While in the car, Rosie opened her toy and played quietly; she also enjoyed the sugary treat, as did Annie.

Home again Anastasia looked back at Rosie and smiled, as she seemed exceedingly happy. A moment was tattooed on her mind. Her little girl just a reminder that this would be a regular challenge for her to take on. She and Dimitri would certainly benefit from taking each kid on their special one-on-one dates occasionally. An investment of their hearts.

Chapter Four

It was a brisk day in the New England countryside. Anastasia sipped her coffee, that which smelled of sugar and tasted like raspberry chocolate candy. She did not like coffee as much as she drank it. But she loved the comfort it brought her. Growing up, Annie woke up to the smell of freshly brewed coffee most mornings.

Her dad, Angus, used coffee as one of his lifelines. He held two jobs and actively participated in raising five children with his wife, Rose. Overwhelmed by life most days, Angus always kept a large mug of coffee on him as a safety blanket. He could take a sip occasionally, which made him feel like taking a deep breath. Up at five a.m. each day and off to his first job, then out by three p.m. and off to do what he called a side job.

He owned a heating and air conditioning business. Then go home to make dinner or pick up after dinner. Then bed by ten p.m., and back to it the next morning. Rose worked some of the years Anastasia was growing up. Most of the later years.

She did not always hold a job in the professional sense, but she did run a daycare for many years. Then back to school to get her Master's in Library Science. Most of the rest of her days, you could find her in a library working. The best librarian Anastasia ever saw. She could also be found behind a computer screen, teaching online classes.

Rose did not see her side as extremely helpful, especially because Angus always worked no matter what Rose chose. But Angus felt her efforts. It warmed his heart when Rose threw herself into anything. To Angus, Rose could do no wrong. He watched his kids grow to respect adults and be incredible people.

When Rose focused on the home, Angus felt this overwhelming, palpable feeling of what "home" really meant. Not just a building but a place filled with love and peace. When Rose focused on cooking, Angus ate like a king. When she focused on cleaning, he came home to a spotless house, and so on. Rose truly had the gift of a great wife and partner through life.

She gave Angus the freedom to do the work and play he needed and wanted. To Angus, life was good. Anastasia wanted so badly to do the same for Dimitri. How she loved him. She feared that he would take her for granted, as her ex-boyfriend Chris had.

When Annie was just eighteen, she met Chris and convinced herself, amongst red flags, that he would be her husband. God ushered her away, but she fought it, wanting to direct her love in some direction, and in everything Chris took her for granted. Annie quit school; Chris hated it. She was isolated from her family; Chris hated it. I tried to become a woman and wife material.

I tried to hold multiple jobs to support them. I tried to pull together friend groups. Tried to throw herself into his family and friends. It did not matter what Annie did; Chris hated it and found ways to punish her for taking steps forward. Anastasia was so innocent and ill-informed about the ways of people and life.

She was so protected from Rose, who saw far too much before she even hit the age of ten. Annie, being a fighter, just thought it meant she needed to deny herself more and fight harder for what she believed in and wanted. If God was not going to help her, then she would do it on her own. That is how Anastasia got here—to CPTSD. She did it on her own, and every time she advanced, Chris would find a way to cut her down.

Until he realized how loyal she was to him. Then he decided he would use her to his benefit. That is when the lessons started. Lessons to distract Anastasia and train her, and if she died doing them well, that would be a win-win for Chris. He started with archery, as he was a savant in it.

He then taught her survival skills: throwing knives, hand-to-hand combat, and at the very end, he broke open the guns. Mostly, he wanted a fan, but as he trained her, she surpassed everything. Even in driving training, she surpassed him. He started to fear what Annie was capable of. Being a sociopath, his brain worked completely differently from everyone else, so he was not used to such feelings.

He started telling Annie, "You are too mean. I cannot marry you. You are too good for me." Anastasia could not believe her ears. Obviously, she was doing something wrong to make him think like that.

She started trying harder to show her love and win his affection once and for all. Anastasia was too young and naïve to understand that she could not make Chris truly be with her, no matter how she willed it. The more she tried to control it, the more she lost herself. Until she was nothing beyond a weapon for Chris to cage up when not in use and unleash when he needed. Anastasia shuddered at the things she had done.

She worried about the things she did not remember. Putting her body in such a state that she would black out. Whatever subconscious was available would take over. Even when she was conscious, she felt she was in a dream world. Everything seemed so easy and hard at the same time.

If she was driving, she would not consider anything dangerous, as nothing could hurt her more than she had already been hurt. The only feeling she could muster upon command or at all was anger. Her rage built up so high that it stomped out every other emotion. She saw everything as without spirit or soul and felt no ill doing what she had to do to get what she needed to be done. She had become her worst enemy.

She had become a sociopath. Life was turned upside-down, and Annie had no worries in the world. She was always on edge anyway. Nothing can destroy someone who has nothing and is only an empty carcass. Someone who prayed for death because she refused to give such a release to herself.

Nope, that was the only area in which she would not play God. For those with CPTSD, have you gotten to this point while in the presence of your attackers to survive and maybe even thrive in a place you thought they needed you to be before finally freeing you? Because in the state of survival, the niceties go out the window. Your captors become your god, and you must do whatever it takes to make it through and get to the other side.

You eat, sleep, breathe, and learn everything and anything about them. You balance out their strengths and your weakness. You look for modes of escape and when the time is right you attack and run. Anastasia, like most victims of sociopathic or psychopathic abuse, could not run far enough. So, she coaxed Chris into a comfortable lull, and then hid in plain sight.

When he came for her to attack, she would have witnesses. They may not understand, but they would and did see what she had been convinced not to show anyone for years. When she was pregnant with Albert, it was time. She took all the responsibility instead of tormenting him with just the thought of a child, then hid in her parents' basement. She continued to go to her jobs and deal with other crappy people she had to threaten.

Going crazy on them as she was planning their deaths by her hand. Later to see one and for her (that person) to better understand. When Albert was born, everything came to a halt. It would be seven weeks into Albert's life that Anastasia would realize how well she had dealt with her sociopathic attacker. Instead of coming to see Albert (for real, not in his ever-present stalking manner that continued to this day), of his own accord, he hid behind a mutual friend Annie called "Butters".

She convinced Anastasia she would come to shower Albert with gifts, but instead Chris came. He stayed for thirty minutes and was unimpressed, calling Albert "the child". That night, he would bring hell back full force, and Anastasia would spend the next year fighting for their lives with someone who lived in the shadows, too scared to come out and fight her. That was when Anastasia reestablished her faith in the God of the universe. She prayed and prayed through tears as she held Albert for what felt like nine months straight.

Then, when Albert was eighteen months old, he finally met Dimitri, his true God-given father. Dimitri met Albert, and instantly he smiled. "It is nice to meet you, Albert," he said as he shook his tiny hand. Albert giggled. They played for two hours, only to end with Dimitri asking about Albert's sperm donor, completely confused as to why he would not want to be a part of this precious little boy's life.

Indeed, Albert was a treasure to Dimitri from day one. Anastasia returned to the cold New England day with a sigh of relief. I praise God for taking her through all of that and bringing her here. Anastasia once again smelled the coffee, heard her babies' voices while they played, and felt the warm, fluffy sweater on her arms. Looking out the window at the sunny blue skies and beautiful hilly terrain.

Chapter Five

Anastasia and Dimitri sat playing cards and chatted. She spoke of her fear of any woman taking him. She once saw only a look come from her ex, and that laid the foundation for all cheating. At that time, she refused to acknowledge it, telling herself he would never do such a thing. Something Chris always used to defend himself.

Yet, there it was every so often, mostly at church. The telling look gave her all she needed to know. Annie thought back to those days as she fought to better understand how she could possibly get through any other church interactions. She knew Dimitri was all she ever wanted and was taught the wrong move would make her lose him. Annie was drawn to doing everything in a relationship and not letting anyone take care of her.

Nor communicating what she needed but pushing past the pain, hoping there would be better. Well, she had done that in relationships in the past. Sure enough, almost every relationship she had ended in cheating. It was not until she went on the quest to find out why all her relationships failed in such a way and why the most prominent was flaunting it in front of her face most of the eight years. She started to realize people need to be needed.

It gives them a reason to stay and to push forward. If a person does not feel needed in any given area, they will assume they can just move on. However this was the exact opposite of what Annie wanted. She thought lessening their load and not burdening them with her feelings and emotions was the answer. When, in fact, it was the antithesis of what the relationship truly needed.

With Dimitri, she refused to fall into the same trap. When she felt herself doing what she was inclined toward, she would put a stop to it. Sometimes the stop was a random explosion, and other times it was a sit-down conversation. These conversations consisted of explaining one's mind, as no one was a mind reader, and delegating tasks. Delegating tasks meant that each person was critical to a smooth transition in any area and certainly necessary in moving forward down the path of life.

Today was about women being interested in Dimitri, which made Anastasia feel like she did not stand a chance of keeping him. She already knew she was not the best at anything and would never be the most gorgeous in any given room. It is impossible to be perfect unless you are God, and Anastasia most certainly was not. She hung her head low as she explained to him where her heart and mind were. As Dimitri always did, he explained to her that she was the one for him and he was the one for her.

As they chatted, Anastasia pulled glimpses of the lines that Dimitri spoke. One, if anything happened to you and the kids, I would go become an orthodox monk and live alone gardening. When we got married, I thought that was a binding contract that we would always be partners in crime and go through life together. Three, you are my constant, so when we fight, I feel lost and like I am floating around looking for the ground. Anastasia began to pray and heard God say, "He is your husband through and through and will be until eighty-two."

Dimitri was standing right in front of her. Communicating with her and contributing to her every day. Rarely did he leave for more than a few days on the obligatory work trips. Even then, he was present through phone and online interfaces. He was most assuredly the best man for her.

She hoped she could continue to be the best woman for him. Though she rarely lets herself believe such things this early on in their relationship. She did not know where time and life would lead them, but she was grateful for this conversation on this day. Annie would reflect on these statements whenever she felt weak and like her husband did not actually want her.

They would become a type of mantra for her bleeding heart. Also, Dimitri's closeness would remind her that he would not be beside her if he did not want to be. Soothing in many ways. A man as madly in love as she was.

Chapter Six

Anastasia sat and thought about how she would prepare for next year's winter. She always had big dreams of canning a bunch of fruits and vegetables. She dreamt of making and maintaining a small greenhouse and putting together quite a lovely garden. One thing held her back: Anastasia lacked follow-through. She would dream big and then fail to take the steps she needed toward her goals.

But this year, she would try again. I just recently found her canning book and learned how to make berry pie fillings and jams. She was one step closer to her dream. Now she knew how to sterilize the cans and what cans to use. She knew she would need to buy many more cans and pickling brine and go step by step in canning each vegetable and fruit when the time came.

But it would be worth it. Their cellar was perfect for taking a portion out to be a root cellar. Now to actually make the garden and greenhouse. Annie liked the idea more than the work. To go out each day and water and take time out to weed.

Nothing worth having comes easily. She wondered if she could master a garden and a greenhouse. Then, through the canning process to preserve everything from sauces to soups, she could save her family a ton of money and health. There was no need to rush into anything, as it was still the dead of winter. She would use store-bought vegetables and fruits this year to learn the canning process.

Then, when spring came, she would be ready to set up her

garden, one step at a time. Anastasia calmed herself before her mind ran off on her. She thought back at the gardens her mom had done during her childhood. Always needing to be moved, but really, Rose had a green thumb. The gardens always flourished, no matter what animals ate the vegetables and the roots.

It was during those years that Annie felt as though they ate like kings. Though by the time Anastasia was old enough to watch, Rose was too busy to do any canning and preserving. Anastasia would grow up and hear stories of those days and wish she could have been a part of it to learn from one of her greatest teachers. But she spent time staring at other women's gardens and listening to them talk about canning and preserving. The closest she got to watch such wonder was an apple cider party at her friend's house in her early twenties.

Anastasia thought it was weird to be driving up to a trailer in the middle of the country with a bunch of land and a barn way bigger than the house, but she did not mind. So many people came to make cider that night. They had a fire, and in the barn, everyone took a turn at the cider press. Anastasia really did not mind going anywhere as long as she was surrounded by friends. Friends meant those that Chris approved of, as he, at that point, did not allow Annie to hang out with anyone else.

She rejoiced in the evening that she and Chris were both happy and preoccupied by their surroundings. Anastasia and Chris made their rounds while the cider was still being pressed. Anastasia realized she needed to use the ladies' room, but the toilet in the trailer was clogged. She went to Chris to tell him, and he felt no rush to rid her of this discomfort. After a while, he said he was ready to go, and Annie should start saying her goodbyes.

Annie was so relieved, as she was embarrassed to tell anyone else. Chris took so long saying his goodbyes that Annie sat with three beautiful little girls who had recently lost their dad in a car accident and read them a story. They listened intently and snuggled up close to Anastasia. Once Chris found out, he came into the trailer as fast as he could and told Annie they needed to leave. How could she get comfortable and win those little girls over without Chris in control?

He was angry. Their mom tried to buy Annie time by chatting with Chris, but Annie knew he had made up his mind. Anastasia jumped in his car and begged him to take her to the bathroom. It was now eleven p.m. in the country, and very few places were open. Chris found Annie in a creepy outhouse next to a closed gas station.

She went into the dark outhouse and realized the door did not close all the way. She held it as she pulled her pants down, and just then Chris decided it would be helpful to put his brights straight at the outhouse. The outhouse was plastic, and Chris got some sick laughs out of watching Annie's silhouette go to the bathroom. When Anastasia got back in the car, she was upset, which made Chris happy. "What did I do this time?"

Taking notes in her mind. "Why would you turn your lights on and flash the outhouse while I peed?"

Chris smiled and said, "I was trying to help, to give you light." Anastasia brushed off her frustration, as it was a long ride home. If she knew anything by now, it was that Chris would do anything to inconvenience her.

If she pitched a fit now, Chris would just leave her in the country to get another ride home. It was dark and too late to go house-calling, so Anastasia looked out the window and closed her mouth. An hour later, Annie arrived home in one piece. That night, Chris decided to ramp up his anger to make sure Annie ended the night in a bad mood. As they pulled into the driveway, he started talking about all the subjects he knew Annie hated.

Then the car came to a stop, and Chris said, "Well, you are being nasty tonight. I think we should break up." Annie was taken aback. She scanned through the night's events, frantically trying to find the thing that made him so upset. She had done all he asked for and was pleasant until the very last minute, even though he took every opportunity to make any disaster happen.

She said, "I will try to be nicer. Please, let's not break up."

"Nope, I have made up my mind. Now get out of my car."

"Please, Chris, I just want to be with you. Please tell me what I need to do."

"I am going to have to take some time to think about whether I can even accept you after what you have done. Now get out." Then he saw it—the thing that filled his bucket. Her tears started to fall as she locked her door.

"No, please, I will do anything." Chris smiled with a sinister smile, and then grabbed her face with his hands. He wiped her tears and looked her in the eye. "Give me time, Anastasia. That's what I need you to do."

Then he reached past her, unlocked it, and opened the door. He got out of the car and walked around to hold her door open, as now Angus had popped his head out of the living room curtains. Chris was a sucker for people's praise. He had a knack for completely crushing Anastasia, and at the same time, he looked chivalrous to the rest of the world. Angus smiled and went to bed.

Anastasia tried to clear her face in case Angus had not truly gone to sleep yet, then got out of the car. Chris slammed the door behind her and said, "So long." Then I drove off. Anastasia shook as she got her keys out of her pocket and opened the side door of her parents' house. She took a few deep breaths, hoping the face of crying would disappear before anyone knew what happened, and she had to lie once more because telling the truth came with repercussions.

Repercussions like having to cut someone else out of her life, getting screamed at, or him disappearing for weeks. Annie would spend the next three weeks texting Chris every day, hoping that day would be the one he talked to her. It would be years before she realized that he was gone; he was with someone else. When that relationship failed or he was over the person, he would come crawling back to the old faithful back burner, Annie. Who had been happy to accept him back no matter what wrongs he had done?

Then he would spend the next part of the relationship trying to be everything he wanted her to be and doing everything right by him. Nothing is right with her. An ever-changing target contradicts its own pattern or flow. Yet he would inevitably leave again. That was their cycle; around and around the Chris Ferris wheel Annie went.

Only to lose more of herself and her life each time; hoping to gain someone who was never worth it in the first place. Looking back, Annie was disgusted with herself. How could she let anyone, especially someone she thought loved her, treat her like this? Compromise is one thing, but giving up all you are is something you should never have to do for love. Even God sent his son to give his life for us to be spotless lambs.

We are not perfect. We are not Jesus Christ. That is not our lot; that was Christ's, and we benefit from the price he paid. Only God himself deserves that type of sacrifice. Anastasia would willingly give her life to the people she loved. After Chris, she made certain they loved and respected her too, every step of the way.

Perhaps overly cautious, but she learned to never let anyone do what he had done to her ever again. You teach people how to love you, not the other way around. God teaches us, and we teach others. When they fail or fall, we dust them off and reiterate that life is meant to be lived. God gave us Americans and Christians the gift of freedom.

No man can put chains on us of their own accord; we need to let them. So do not let them. Only God is our judge. Anastasia realized this was likely why she had a gap between dreaming of canning and actually canning. But the only way to truly grow is through prayer and God's healing and guidance. Anastasia was ready to take the next step with her God-given husband, Dimitri. To push past her pain to do her part in proving Dimitri loved and respected Annie and vice versa. It was time to let go of the past and drive forward in this area with God as her guide.

Chapter Seven

Anastasia and the kids set out to rid their trunk of the giveaway items; it held far too long. Annie called it "an adventure" when she took the kids out to try to make everything feel magical. But today, the word "adventure" lives up to its definition. They stopped at the local Goodwill, which took her bags but refused to take her baby stuff. The employees pointed her toward the local Once upon a Child store.

She only took one of the three items she had left. Anastasia asked what could be done with the others, only to hear about the Salvation Army, which was down the road. At the Salvation Army, their baby stuff was turned away. Annie then drove to the local shelter to see if she could drop off the items left. Only to look from a distance and see what looked like zombified druggies hovering around the door.

She knew too well what drugs did to a person and refused to let her kids come into contact with such things at their ripe ages. She decided to drive off, hoping she would get another chance that week to drop off the rest of the items. While she was at Once Upon a Child waiting for the items to be priced, Annie played I spy with Albert, Rosie, and Scott. They giggled as Rosie and Albert took turns choosing things, and Scott rested. "I spy with my little eye something green," said Albert.

Annie was in a daze, wondering how long it would take to push through the few things she had brought in. She saw a woman in a military uniform walking into the store to drop off some items. Anastasia was excited at first to see a military woman. Then something hit her. A deep-rooted feeling with no context.

She started feeling gross inside, with anger and resentment toward Dimitri. At first, she was taken aback, then she realized why she felt this way. Chris liked to keep tabs on Anastasia. He needed to see her daily, and he also took pleasure in having multiple sexual partners at any given time. He would use these women to keep tabs on Annie by telling them some sob stories.

Some were cool and tried to take her under their wing like a prostitute he collected from his tirades. Roxie was chubby and had long blonde hair. She liked cocaine, and she used her body to get what she wanted. "Annie, what you need to do is get a few guys who pay your bills in exchange for sex, and then you will really be living." Every time Roxie saw Annie, she made it her mission to tell her of all the wealthy and eligible bachelors in the room.

Annie giggled when she took her under her wing, and in those moments, it made her feel like all the pain she went through with Chris was worth it. This woman saw her and truly wanted to help her. It was a glimpse of sunshine in such a dark situation. Yes, a glimpse of sunshine from a drug addict hooker who wanted to make Annie just like her. I even tried to get Anastasia to sign up for pole dancing classes.

She still giggled when she thought of Roxie, prayed for her, and thanked God for her. Today, this feeling had nothing to do with Roxie. It had to do with those other girls who would randomly pop up to check on Anastasia for Chris.

Chris liked to bug her car and phones. One day she slept at Chris' apartment, and while she slept, he switched out her phone memory card. With these items, he knew where she was and when she was there. The girls were just to flex his power and try to stir up Anastasia's feelings.

Chapter Eight

The first few times Annie thought these women were just friends and enjoyed the company, but after a while, she realized what it was. Chris's favorite thing to do was put his sex partners in the same room and see how they reacted toward each other. The only difference was that they all knew about Annie; she did not know about them. This was his way of planting friends around Annie.

Then anything she said went back to him. One of them felt so bad that he had done so much wrong that she spent hours driving back and forth while Annie was pregnant to keep her company. It took a few months, but finally she admitted that Chris had cheated on Annie with her and that she was keeping Chris up to date on how the pregnancy was going. Anastasia was seven months pregnant with Albert at the time. She remembered being in the movie theater parking lot after they went to see a movie together.

The same theater where she found out about another girl he cheated with years before they never told her. Her and ten friends went to see a movie that just came out. A James Bond movie, and at midnight, they all circled around the parking lot. As people started to peel away the girl, Amy looked and pointed at Chris and said, "You better make sure I get home tonight."

Anastasia was struck and asked Chris, to which he said, "I do not know what she meant." Under a sinister smile. Getting the rise he wanted out of Anastasia and getting Amy, as well as seemingly at the moment Anastasia blessed the relationship. Even after all of that, she convinced herself that Chris loved her and only wanted to be with her, and that was just some fluke. Anastasia would continue to answer for Chris and bring less and less up because when she did, he would scream at her, call her crazy, and then the ultimate punishment of silence for however long he felt was right.

To Annie, Chris was everything. To Chris, Annie was the shit stuck to the bottom of his shoe he could not seem to get rid of. No matter how much he stomped on it or tried to wipe it off on sharp objects, it just stayed there. So, he would take his shoes off from time to time and put different ones on. Then, when he was ready to put the shit shoes back on, he contacted her again.

He only wore them when life had become dull and boring, and he wanted to have some fun with someone completely willing and resilient. Anastasia worshipped Chris. She defended him from herself and everyone else. She let him know her name, telling people she was the person he was. He would act like he learned from her personality to get what he wanted from people.

Anastasia was all too willing to give him lessons, as any attention from Chris was her biggest addiction. He was her drug. Near the end of their two-point five-year relationship (though they met up each year and got back together until he found someone else and dumped her again—eight years total), Chris would take every opportunity to get Annie in a compromising position with her friends (the friends he put around her) to make her look like the person he swore she was. The day he officially broke up with her, Anastasia drove two hours to see him.

He told her to meet him at a Taco Bell. Taco Bell was his metaphor for Annie. He once wrote a story about Taco Bell cheating on it with Del Taco and how he knew it was wrong and would not do it again. The taco bell was the best. He read it to Annie and gave it to her to keep.

At the time, she thought it was just a school project. It would take years for her to realize what he did and was trying to say. This day, she went to Taco Bell in hopes of rekindling their broken relationship. He made her sit there for 45 minutes, waiting for him to answer the question of whether they were still together. He waited until a mutual friend showed up.

Then I looked at her and said, "No, I could not be with you. You are too mean and definitely not wife material." Anastasia was crushed. Chris smiled and ran to the friend, urging him to come talk with Annie. Joe came over, excited to see Anastasia.

"We are going to a movie if you would like to come!" Anastasia half smiled, trying to hide her sadness, which made Chris angry.

Anastasia said, "Maybe another time, Joe; thank you. It was nice to see you too." Chris angrily brought Joe back to his car.

"Well, Joe, I will meet you there." Joe drove off, and Chris came back to dig the knife in.

"Why did you have to be so mean to Joe? That was rude, Annie. I cannot believe you would do that to him. You know what? Just go. I was going to reconsider my choice if you came to the movie, but you obviously want to go, so just go. Do not talk to me for a while; I need time to figure things out. Now I am running late for the movie I promised I would be at, and it's all your fault. If you had not dragged me out here, I would be there now. Bye Annie. I do not want to see your face any more. You are such a horrible person. Just bye."

With that, Chris got in his car, watching Annie intently as she put her head down and sat crushed in her car. She considered whether she should spend the last of her money to get home or to go to the movie, and she hoped someone would pay for her gas. She drove home twenty minutes later and never regretted that decision.

Chapter Nine

Nothing makes you feel more alone than running from God. God surrounds us on all sides, and when we try to run, there is a palpable difference for believers. Hiding comes in a close second. Then there is throwing your all into one person and refusing to accept help or creature comforts you have run to in hard times of the past. Anastasia always thought she would live in her hometown.

After the dreams of traveling were crushed by naysayers, Annie put more stock in her own feelings and desires. She figured being in the small town of Willow sport was her lot. So many memories rushed back while she drove the back roads she took daily to work or school for the past ten years. She loved these backcountry roads. Many rides were devoted to her screaming, crying and praying.

For Annie, she felt more of a bond to these roads than she did to anyone around her. She learned long ago to hold people loosely as she went through a mass series of deaths among friends and family. She became more and more numb. Then, after she met Chris, he completely repacked her friend group with people he approved of and no one else. She let go of the idea that she could never really have loyal people around her; even some of her family members felt disloyal.

But these roads were here for Anastasia whenever she needed a shoulder to cry on. She could drive until she could no longer see through the tears, and then she would pull to the shoulder and let it all out. Roads that had many outlets to anywhere she wished to go, which could also give her the adventure her heart craved. Some days, Annie would drive for hours.

Sometimes all she needed was a few minutes. Today Annie felt extremely sick; she felt as though Dimitri was lying to her or omitting information. Her body broke down considering how badly he wanted to go on this next weeklong trip. He kept telling her over and over that he did not want to, but kept pushing for it. From there alone, Anastasia was on edge.

She took a deep breath and closed her eyes. She would handle Dimitri later, but for now, she imagined those roads. Instead of her ritzy Tahoe, Dimitri urged her to get; she was back in her crappy old stick shift Aveo coop. Windows rolled down manually, but not too low because the locks had fallen into the drivers and copilots' doors. Her head almost touched the ceiling as she sat up straight and tall, which made her giggle a little even now.

Every stop and start was completely under her control. It was a summer day with grass, blue skies, and sun. She had Hercules in the back of the car, waiting patiently for her portion to be done so he could have his walk in the park. If only she could go back to that moment, not just in her mind. Annie thought about Hercules a bit longer, then shut the memory down as she started to cry.

"No more turmoil today. Thank you, Hercules, for being ours. I miss you." Anastasia loved to take Hercules to the park when he was alive. She trained him to stick with her, off the leash, so he could be free.

If he got into a dangerous situation, she would save him. This gave him an air of fearlessness. It was this training that taught him later to do the same thing for the dogs around him. Always coming to the aid and rescue of a deaf and blind dog who would get out of his house and then get lost. Hercules was a true gem.

He had his bad moments overall; he was such a treasure, and Annie desperately missed him. She thought regularly about getting a pet other than the chickens Dimitri talked her into. When she tried to help Marie rescue a dog at the beginning of her marriage with Dimitri, she almost died of a heart attack. Dimitri drove to help pick up the dog but did nothing else. Being pregnant with an infant and a toddler to take care of and train a very wild, powerful dog was not something Annie could do.

Sometimes Dimitri felt like a little kid with his tantrums. Not that Annie did not have many tantrums herself. Usually, Dimitri's consisted of leaving Annie alone for a few hours to fight for her kids and whatever else. He would just run to work when things got too hard, and that's where he left her today. Off to work, Annie, still sick from a pandemic virus with three sick children and now on her period, was so overwhelmed she could not see straight.

When her head was not spinning, it hurt. She recalled Dimitri urging her to use her spare cash recently as well. There were so many offenses to build against him today, as she knew his trip was looming over her head, and yet again, she would be left alone with absolutely no help for a week. Most of his trips she has tried to power through, but right now she finds she is too tired to even consider what will be done.

Too tired to even consider getting through today. Dimitri is also sick; trying to keep his job does not help. Annie was angry, that's all. Very angry.

As angry as little Scott sounded as he cried in his crib, Annie decided it would be better to join and feed him. They were both hurting. Maybe together they would feel the comfort they so desperately needed.

Chapter Ten

Anastasia listened to Sara Bareilles in the background as she chopped vegetables to make an overdue chicken rice soup. A song resonated with her from her album for the musical Waitress. Actually, most of the songs on the album resonated with Annie. Sara Bareilles was indeed a poet, and Annie loved how deep most of her songs were. She could particularly feel her heart pouring into this song today: "Most days I don't recognize me. But these shoes and this apron-that place and its patrons have taken more than I gave them. It's not easy to know I'm not anything like I used to be. Although it's true…" Annie sang along, breathing in the words that felt so much like home for the past few years. If no one else understood, Sara did.

That made Annie feel less alone, even just for the duration of the song. Then she thought of the reason the musical, movie, and album were made and how many people truly felt they could relate, even to pieces of it had become the rage in New York City and elsewhere for some time since this particular album was made.

That made Anastasia feel even less alone. She started to hum as her mind trailed off. How many people, at least once in their lives, let someone take advantage of them? Not even uprooting them, per se, but simply letting them get one over on them. Letting them lie to their faces, whether they knew it or not, and accepting it?

Our society has become too soft. People are scared to fight back and defend their boundaries-God, country, and families.

Annie thought of the warriors sitting out on the front lines. She considered the movies she saw of men sitting in trenches waiting to be told to attack. Men go through buildings or walk streets only to be shot at and need to take cover.

Men came down from helicopters into a hot zone because they were told it was their duty and those people were the enemy. Yet the people at the top were the ones pulling the strings from a safe distance. Take Hitler, for example. When World War II started, Hitler was just a young soldier. He went to war and did what he was told.

It's likely he saw too much, and his leaders refused to advance his career because he was too crazy. After a time in prison writing a book, *Mein Kompf*, Hitler was released. The war ended, and Germany was laden with the debt of most countries' contributions; this put them in dire straits. The socialist party seemed to want to help the people. Hitler saw this as his chance to fulfill the dreams outlined in his book.

He was likeable and charismatic, and the people believed he wanted good for them. But a person so abused would trust anyone who said they would help. Hitler did fulfill his goals, and the German people and most of Europe had to pay. Those people who backed him had to do unspeakable things. If they went soft or gave up, he would kill their families or send them to the frontlines during the rage of war to die for the cause.

All seems normal until you find out that Hitler never set foot in a concentration or extermination camp. Nope, he was the puppeteer of those working in the camps. Enough to streamline the process and fulfill his goals without getting his hands dirty. Forcing people who trusted him to die or do what no person should have to do Even Stalin killed more than Hitler and used Hitler's regime to hide what he was doing.

Stalin killed anyone who opposed him and would sign papers with the names of countrymen who were to be killed. He starved for the rest. It would take years for the world to realize what had happened. Millions, maybe billions, of people died at his pen—paper signature, never allowing his hands to get dirty. Anastasia looked around at society now.

A muted America hung in the balance as politicians fought for money and power instead of God, the people, and the country. They became muckrakers and kept coming onto the television, telling people they were for them. They just needed to do this to stay in their good graces. They gave resources to other enemy countries and lied to the people they were supposed to be representing and supporting. She thought about Chris and how familiar this all felt.

This time, she was not alone in the abuse. No, the entire American population, not just her or the soldiers who fought for the freedom they believed in. They really risked their lives for politicians who wished to play God. All the people of America were under the sociopathic abuse by their so-called "government for them". That government sought to divide, just like they have for many years.

The early-onset steps of genocide Anastasia had done extensive research on genocides. She felt a lurking suspicion that the powers at hand, were trying to form divisions in small advances toward genocide. The first stop to conquering is to divide and create propaganda. It seemed to Annie that the government was not seeking to help the people but simply to conquer and abuse them.

She prepared for the day they would get exactly what they wanted, not knowing what that was. Yet simultaneously, she prayed to the real God. The God who created all in the beginning and the end. The God who opened up the ground and swallowed people See, when people play God, they forget there is a true God watching, and when he wants and wills it, he will pull the plug.

Look at Satan, the chief musician, but he got greedy,

abusive, and overall wanted to be God. When the time was right, God sent him packing. Though he rules this earth currently, which is why all these things are coming to fruition, there will be a time when God, Jesus Christ, the Holy Spirit, and their angels will bring the real fine. Not just the wimpy fire of Satan and his demons.

God has and always will be the Father who is in control; nothing compares to the holy trinity. While we as a community of people suffer through the abuses of the current society, it is important to remember who you serve. To re-establish your faith and respect for Him and get ready for Him to come in the eleventh hour to blow us all away. Some good, some bad. Anastasia rejoiced at these thoughts.

She looked crazy as she lifted her fists in the air and yelled, "Amen!" But she knew she was not wrong. I was reminded of the story of the woman who was praying at the temple silently, and the priest thought she was crazy and sent her home. Her prayers were answered because it was all God's will. So today we suffer together, and as much as the powers at hand wish to divide the people, it is their pestering abuse that will bind us together.

Every person suffers together, and when you suffer together, your bond is unbreakable. Anastasia knew this was one of the reasons for the isolation portion. But isolate a people, and they will have time, which society cannot afford, to realize what is truly happening. One by one, each unit will grow stronger.

Then, when they are back together, instead of a small puddle, it will be an ocean that confronts these puppet masters playing God. Waiting to strike until the perfect moment. Anastasia smiled and thought of Noah's Ark. "It will be a glorious day, indeed glorious, a day for the kingdom of God."

Chapter Eleven

Anastasia had a lovely lunch with Dimitri. He smiled and made faces to show her how much he enjoyed the egg salad sandwich she made. This was the best reward for her cooking, and Dimitri knew Annie felt that way. He would muster up his enthusiasm while she prepared any food. Then let it shine to encourage her to cook more.

This was balanced by the comments, "Sometimes you cook amazing food, and sometimes it is a complete failure." Anastasia stayed humble but knew every good woman needed to strive to feed her family. She took it all in stride. Sometimes she would ask Dimitri for tips or watch how he cooked, as he was an expert at cooking meals. He made restaurant-quality meals. Man could cook Dimitri!

Anastasia loved his dishes. It was rare for her to turn down his cooking. When she was growing up, she ate mostly pasta and potatoes. These dishes were easy bulk meals and hardy enough to fill hers and her family's stomachs for cheap. Though Annie loved pasta and potatoes, she also loved the Mediterranean infusion diet Dimitri pulled together from his years as an adult.

His mom and dad both were great cooks, so when he became an adult, he had to learn for himself. He took skills from them and lessons he learned online and made his own special style of cooking. Anastasia listened as Scott cried, waking abruptly from his nap. Albert had been singing too loud, and Scott got scared. She remembered when Albert was Scott's age.

He cried what felt like constantly one night as she lay him in the bassinet, bundled in more layers than any baby needs. She fell asleep beside him as he cried. Anastasia tuned out the cry after checking his diaper, feeding him, and making sure he was safe in his bassinet. It was no secret that Chris had been sneaking in at different times. Never truly approaching an awake Anastasia but always staying in the shadows until she was asleep. Anastasia slept so deeply that she had not slept in months; she barely slept at that time.

She had a dream she took as a prophecy. Within her dream, she woke up to a dead Albert in the bassinet with pierced ears. She cried in the dream, and then woke up panicked, tears streaming down her face. She looked in the bassinet and felt Albert's chest. A trick was taught to her by her oldest sister-in-law.

A deep sigh of relief came out of Annie as she found Albert alive. He was sleeping soundly beside her. Moments later, he woke up crying again. At the time, Annie did not know that Albert was likely hungry, and she cried so much because of that. She fed him breastmilk as much as possible but did not know it was likely not enough.

So, she would pray and walk him while rocking him. It was not until he started eating solids (pureed) that he cried less. That was a very relieving time for Annie. After months of constant crying and little sleep, that day, she threw out the bassinet and had Albert sleep on top of her until he was nine months old.

It was only a week later that they were sleeping. Albert is face down in Anastasia's arms, surrounded by pillows to keep him above Anastasia and her breasts readily available for him (thus the face down). She slept as soundly as is possible when there is a precious child sleeping on you. All the sudden, Albert started crying out of a sound sleep. Anastasia woke up to him crying a few moments later.

When she examined him, she found his sleeper had been unbuttoned, as had his onesie. His diaper was disheveled, and Albert cried as Anastasia changed his clothes. She was so upset that she did not think to look around the room or floor of the house she was in. That never happened before, and it never happened again after that. Anastasia threw out all the button sleepers until he was old enough to at least express what happened.

He looked like he was ready for sleep at all times of the day. But Anastasia never wanted whatever happened that night to happen again. Scott's crying subsided, and he fell back asleep. Albert and Rosie kept quietly playing in their rooms. Trying to stay quiet enough not to disturb Scott.

Rosie and Scott were so lucky to be born with Dimitri around. They never had to deal with the fear Albert felt in his first year of life. Because of that, they were overall much mellower children. It was not until Albert moved into Dimitri's home that he felt truly safe and like he could finally thrive. Since then, he has grown so brave and bold that he challenges both Anastasia and Dimitri from time to time.

Something he would not have done had he not met his dad Dimitri. For quite some time, Albert feared most things. Particularly baseball caps. One morning he woke up scared of them, when he had not had the fear before. Albert has grown out of this fear and many others, and he may never remember these times. Anastasia prayed he would not.

However, Annie would never forget. That night, Chris had broken in and hovered over Albert's crib; he was wearing a baseball cap. Albert recognized him, but Chris had been drinking and tried to hurt Albert to get back at Anastasia. Albert cried loudly for Anastasia, who came running into the dark room. By the time she got there, Chris was in hiding again.

Annie grabbed Albert; she could smell the alcohol in the air. She took Albert upstairs with her, then checked the house before letting him lay back down in the crib. By that time, she had already put screws in the windows so Chris could not enter through them. She also had a deer cam, Angus, set up outside her window. She had a motion light outside her door, and she knew after that night that Chris must have had the keys she lost when she went into labor.

Anastasia pleaded with Angus and Rose to change the locks on all the doors. After some griping, they did just that. Though Chris would still torment Annie by setting off the motion light and using a flashlight to shine into her window repeatedly through the nights, at least Albert was safe. He could not get inside.

Anastasia held Albert close to her that year. Far too close. She knew only she could truly protect him from Chris. It was comfortable until she realized Chris had won over Philip and Tajkia, Anastasia's brother and sister-in-law.

When they were alone with Albert, they would bring him to the woods at the side of the house to give Chris a chance to see him. Chris ate it up, playing the victim card. He got to act like he wanted Albert to win Philip's and Tajkia's favor in the same breath, making Anastasia look like a monster. They were so blinded that Tajkia stole the house keys and gave Chris a copy to come in anytime he wanted. Chris started coming regularly again.

So, Anastasia moved her and Albert to an apartment on the second story of an apartment complex. All with Dimitri's help.

Even there, Chris found them. He made friends with her downstairs neighbors and used them to try to punish Annie for having Albert. Because of their chain-smoking, Albert and Anastasia had to rush to the hospital as Albert could not breathe.

He almost died that night. At times, they helped but were mostly regarded as enemies of Anastasia. It was not until the following fall that Annie realized the connection. Chris came in with a crew, and as Annie left with Albert, she heard his voice say, "Yeah, I know she looks nice, but she won't even let me see my own kid." Anastasia brushed it off and kept walking, praying that would be the end of it.

By Thanksgiving, Albert and Anastasia were forced back into Angus and Rose's house. By that time, Dimitri and Rosie were part of the picture. Dimitri deployed to Eastern Europe but was extremely present, and Rosie was growing in Anastasia's stomach. Chris was taken aback and worried about what would happen if he crossed Dimitri and his contacts, so he eased up. Months later, Dimitri, Annie, Rosie, and Albert moved into Dimitri's home.

Hours away from Chris. Even still, in the summers, Chris, who found out the address from his ever-loyal friend Philip, would drive by on his dirt bike each week. Some days he would get bored and mess with Annie and Dimitri, but mostly he would stay away. Still, Anastasia was always ready to take out the trash. When she got her chance to take out this trash, she would take her time, do it right (so he never came back), and enjoy the torture portion far too much.

However she had gotten much softer and more emotional because Dimitri was so good to her, she knew how to turn it off and turn it back into the weapon Chris and her teachers had trained her to be. This time, she would not let Chris go away unscathed. Therefore, he hid in the shadows. Anastasia no longer needed anything from him, and Dimitri was also to be feared. Dimitri had no connection other than knowing he was a horrible person. Thus, the night at Dave and Buster's arcade.

Chapter Twelve

She needed to ward him off, but if he came to her turf face to face, she would see that as war. Stalkers drive by, sitting in a public place where there are too many eyes. Anastasia could do very little but come to her home, like he came to her parents, and she would be ready. She did not want to be like this any more.

So many years of fighting the pain of hurting someone else but nothing would stand Anastasia down if it came to her miracles. She would easily die to save her husband and children. But to rush at a narcissistic sociopath like a bull would only excite him more.

She was grateful to have another day to strategize. He was prayerful and hopeful that the longer he waited, the less likely he would be to continue to threaten her life. Chris liked to take everything from Annie. The more she had, the more she feared losing. She knew two things: what she would do to Chris would kill her or send her to prison.

She certainly wanted to avoid such things if she had the choice. Back and forth, she debated this fictitious moment in her life. The moment he would come out of the shadows and give her a chance to do what he had done to her for years, she realized she had drifted too far into the alternate reality again and started to look around to find something to refocus her. Thinking of her husband on the phone, the blood slowly dripping from her vagina, and the coldness of the day touching her toes and nose.

Deep breath in and then out, Anastasia started looking at her surroundings more closely now. One of Rosie's jackets hung on the doorknob of the French doors that divided the living room and playroom. The light from the sun shining through the window created shapes on the ground. The wood is covered with a soft rug. On the rug sat a toy airplane her son Scott got that Christmas.

She looked over to see the probiotics she tried to force Dimitri to take. Now she had a charge. She knew once he got off his important work call, she would once again try to convince him to take his probiotic. She pointed. Dimitri giggled and gently caressed her cheek. "I will take those later."

"Why not now?" He refused to reply and just comedically traipsed away. Anastasia loved Dimitri. She finally, after almost three years, gave herself the chance to open up to loving him with a portion of her heart, which she had held back for so long. Each different moment, God healed her, unlocked another portion of her heart and mind, and available and present to love her family even more.

Grateful to God for such a stubborn, understanding husband, Anastasia smiled and said, "Thank you, God. Thank you so very much. I am unworthy. Please teach me to love him like you have loved him. I give him, our children, and myself to you. Please use us as conduits to glorify you. Love you, God!"

Chapter Thirteen

Anastasia sat in church. This church was much different than what she was used to. The first few Sundays she went, she was completely confused. Now, a year later, she follows along with most things. She had grown to love her priest and Presbytera.

They had formerly been Presbyterian but changed to Greek Orthodox and serve the community extremely well. She certainly felt akin to those two worshippers and servants of the Lord. It was they who made her feel at home in this church. She is similar in age to her parents and is extremely intelligent. They had similar genius quirks as Anastasia.

She found comfort in conversations with each of them and sought to grow and expand their love however she could. Indeed, this Greek Orthodox Church, as strange as it may be, was the perfect spiritual home for Anastasia. On Sunday morning, she sang in the choir. The choir was sparse, and every voice counted. Annie loved to sing, though she struggled because of all her illnesses throughout the years.

She put her best foot forward, the best she had for each service, and served God with her heart. Through this, she felt she had seen many blessings. Anastasia thought back to her churches throughout her life. She started at a Presbyterian church her parents attended. Annie remembered being in the daycare/nursery of the church and playing with the toys.

She was only three when she had her first real memory. At that church, she went to Sunday school, and while in the sanctuary, her parents sat with an old couple on the balcony. She remembered the brass band that served the community at the time and running around the church that felt as though it never ended. When Annie was in sixth grade, her mom decided to change churches. She would visit a different one each Sunday until she found the one she liked the most.

Calvary Chapel. Rose loved to hear Henry teach. He had a mellow voice and was well read. When they joined, it was packed, and the church took place in an apartment building. Soon the church split, and they moved to a building they had built.

The building was simple and nice. The church members took turns helping to build the church on their time off. It would take years to bring to this church all they had in the apartment building, but in time that all came. Anastasia loved to serve at Calvary. She took every opportunity.

Annie served in the children's ministry and on the sound team. She was a part of the youth group and served at fundraiser dinners. She loved her church family and was deeply drawn to them. Her and Marie frequented youth retreats at a missionary's castle near their home, Calvary. Anastasia loved the castle.

It was in the mountains and made of stone. The view and architecture were extremely beautiful. She found herself praying for each retreat to go according to God's will. It was at this Sibley castle that she re-invested in her walk with Christ. Oh, how she loved the serenity and escape the church brought.

Her youth pastor, Daniel, made up the best games and sports and completely transformed the experience. Kristiana, his wife, ministered to the young women. Anastasia wanted to be just like her. Steady was the word she would use to describe Kristiana. She was tall, gorgeous, and stoic.

Annie loved to learn from her whenever she had the

opportunity. Those retreats, in many ways, helped to redefine life for Annie. When she went to college, she joined a few groups and fell away from Calvary. She soon became the president of campus ambassadors at her first college. Again, she served where she could and was always focused on giving the people an awesome experience.

So, they would come back and worship God more. It was during election time that she met Chris. When he found out she was a Christian, he jumped on it. Instead of going with her to her events, he decided it was best that she see his churches. He went to southern Baptist churches.

The pastors would scream, jump up and down, and hit things. They were not all bad, but after a few years of Chris's abuse, Anastasia completely abandoned Calvary and went full-time as an ambassador on. She attended these churches that Chris wanted her to and they would most assuredly give her panic attacks. To which Chris did not care. He felt no need to help Anastasia through such things.

Then watching her suffer made his heart soar like an eagle. If he found she did not panic, he would do whatever he could to make her panic. And certainly, I did not let her get relief from sermons. One day he even took her to an unknown church; she had no idea where they were, and he told her it would be romantic. They sat in the front row to watch Fireproof, a famous Christian romance.

As they watched, Annie heard saws turn on in the basement. Chris was not at all surprised, and when Annie urged him to leave, he begrudgingly listened but made her wait until he was ready. This was common for Chris. He drove and made Annie wait until he was ready to go, no matter where they went. At the end of the night, right before the movie ended, he granted her wish and left with her.

He drove her home, making fun of her as she sat in the passenger seat, trying to figure out what just happened. Years would go by, and she would start attending yet another church he joined to meet girls. This was a relaxing, non-denominational church. The pastor was well-red and mellow. Anastasia had a few problems, so, of course, Chris ramped it up.

He had girlfriends attend and even had Anastasia cater to them. She hated these things, but when you decide to be with someone, you do what you must. Today, Anastasia does not tolerate other women around her man. Back then, she was desperate to have Chris. Dimitri, thankfully, had different vices.

Indeed, this church was the first church that Anastasia had been able to attend without fear. A year ago, she entered the doors, scared of what she would face. Surely, she was not safe in any church from abuse, backlash, and servanthood. It took more time than even today to stop having panic attacks. She would become breathless at different times and be unable to sing.

Or her mind would drift off. But here she was, surrounded by older adults who gave very little thought to her place. They knew they needed her to some extent and were therefore nice enough. They allowed her to sit in her own pew (after trying to move her up and her obviously panicking). They began to accept any quirks, as they had all been beaten down by life from time to time.

Anastasia stayed as consistent and present as possible, working around Dimitri's schedule. She was happy to finally have a place where she could worship the Lord, be around other adults, and help in small ways as she connected. Much less responsibility than she had in the past. In college, she became so driven to help and serve that she lived in a discipleship house, served in two Christian groups, and went to church on Sundays at yet another church. Her life had become serviceable.

Which is why Chris felt the need to breakdown her joy and drive in that area? He figured he could take this opportunity to destroy her in front of people. And show them her true colors. To become her god and have her serve him as diligently as she served the one true God.

Dimitri did not struggle in the same way. He stayed with the kids while Anastasia served in the choir. He also urged her to join the choir because he knew she loved to sing and needed more adult time. This was the kind of man Dimitri was to her.

Anastasia counted herself lucky and blessed. To go from Chris to Dimitri took a long road, but she ended up with the most fitting man for her. She prayed they would be able to always be together. That God would give them the strength to always stay true to each other and Him, one day at a time.

Chapter Fourteen

One day, one breath, one moment. And let God lead instead of leading and controlling. Should I worship Dimitri? Keep your boundaries this time; make him respect and love you. Each day was a battle not to fall face down before him and serve him.

Anastasia looked at Dimitri and knew she wanted to do this right. Not just to love him but to let him and make him truly love her, the way God loves her. Anastasia trained Chris to treat her that way, and because of who he was, he embraced every moment. Dimitri had the ability to do the same, though instead he found he did not want to do that to Annie. When she gave him hints and information to love her, he did it with all he had.

He fought off his fears about abandoning Anastasia and tried to give her the best life possible. Seeing her blossom meant the world to him, and he would fight off his selfish inner child for each moment he could see her light up. Today he sat organizing the items in his closet. As he looked at her reading on the bed with her ice cream on her chest, he relished her presence. Anastasia was not much of a cuddler or very good with emotions in general.

Her past had marred her delight in such things. But seeing her like this was the love language she sent to him. To be close but not too close. Dimitri was sure she was the one his heart would forever love as she smiled over at him. He did not know how he was so lucky to catch his very own Psyche.

She was wanted by so many men, and yet she chose him. On

he went, organizing his things. Items for the closet that once only held his belongings. It was not long ago that he finally relinquished the piece of the closet he had been holding onto, thinking she would inevitably leave him. It had not been long since he rushed home on the first day back to work, worried he would not catch her as she packed her things and ran out the door. Unlike his most prominent ex's, Anastasia did not run.

She told him she felt grounded by his steadiness and confidence. Dimitri tried to understand where she saw that in him as he only saw chaos. He spent his life trying to juggle so many things that even his heart started to fail him. Two years in a row, he had a heart attack, got cellulitis, and almost lost his job. Yet she stayed.

Every time she said, "As long as you do not cheat or abuse me, I will stay, and we will work through anything together." He was astonished at such words, as he had never heard them come from anyone before. Life had been lonely, to say the least. But here he was, focused on his hobby, as his sweet Annie waited for him to finish. To say he felt healthy was an overstatement.

Sure, he had the pandemic flu all over again. But something inside brought peace. Maybe it was the woman patiently awaiting his return to their shared bed. The woman who had decided she would do just that should wait for him. Encouraging him toward his goals and reminding him regularly how lucky she was to have him.

Maybe it was the kids sleeping silently in their rooms, filling up the house he bought with faith that one day he would come to this place. Maybe it was God who never gave up on him. Or the job that so badly yearned for his approval on anything moving forward. But tonight, amidst the beckoning sickness, he felt peace. He embraced the feeling for a moment as he closed his eyes and praised God for what He had brought him.

A life he never knew was possible but had faith would come to pass. A family he had always wanted. A steady job that paid the bills even in this time of economic turmoil. A wife who would silently stand by his side through whatever may come, cheering him on and praying over him. Dimitri felt lucky, if only for a moment, that finally he had all he had worked for.

It seemed like a lifetime to get here. Yet now he was here, soaking up the moments he could. I am still feeling the ever-present chaos of juggling so many pins in the air. He looked up once more and took a moment to embrace the beauty his wife was. "Yup, I am a lucky man."

Chapter Fifteen

Monday came like a flash of lightning. Dimitri was supposed to travel but was deemed sick by the state and told to stay home for five days from his test date. Anastasia was excited to have him home, as she and the kids would have had to say goodbye for a week. Dimitri was excellent at staying in touch with his phone on all occasions. But there was still a void when he was not physically present.

He went out to the store for some supplies as Anastasia sat at home and had her much-needed quiet time while the children rested. Anastasia thought back through her pregnancies. With Scott, Dimitri took a few short trips but was home most of the pregnancy. He worked ten-hour days regularly, but Anastasia felt it more when he was traveling, as she dreaded sleeping without him the most. Even when he went out for the evening, she found herself dreading going to bed without him by her side.

One day during her pregnancy with Scott, he left for a trip, and she broke down, starting to cry uncontrollably. She tried and tried but could not make herself stop crying. That morning, Dimitri left for a weeklong trip before she woke up. They had planned for weeks to do this, but for some reason, when the day came, Annie could not pull herself together. Dimitri was perfectly fine and had been faithful throughout, but something deep inside screamed at her.

She sat on the bathroom floor with Rosie and Albert, with Scott still inside her, and wept. She called Angus and Rose, trying to hide her sobbing, and Rose adamantly suggested she come to be with them. Anastasia got everyone in the car and drove for two hours for comfort and company. On the way there, the tears were set at bay, and she was able to feel hope again. Albert and Rosie are no longer worried for their mom.

As Anastasia tried to analyze that time, the only thing she could tie it to was past pregnancies. She dug deeper. As she dug, she added that it hurt her heart every time she saw Dimitri leave. She dreaded waking up in the mornings with him because, even though they had tons of fun, watching him walk out the door would always put her in a bad mood. During Rosie's pregnancy, Anastasia worked.

Dimitri was deployed. He deployed the day he found out about Rosie. He urged Anastasia to meet up, as they were fresh in their relationship and lived a few hours from each other. She was sure of the fact that she was pregnant with his baby. Dimitri finally had everything he ever dreamt of, and as he sat there, tears streamed down his face.

How ironic that he had all he dreamt of and had to say goodbye for almost a year. He told Anastasia that she did not need to wait for him and could start a life with another man. Although, when he got home, he would find her and his baby and be as present as possible. Anastasia thought about how stupid Dimitri must be. She was so disillusioned to think she could even act like she wanted another person.

She had wanted Dimitri since the first day they met, and no time or distance would change that. Only her convincing herself that the love was not real would change that. But to her, Dimitri was beyond her wildest dreams. He was and still is her miracle man. She laughed as he cried and said, "I won't be giving you up that easily."

They said their goodbyes after a nice breakfast and walked by the Riverside. Dimitri deployed to Eastern Europe for eight months. He traveled to a handful of different countries and still did not take even a day off from contacting Annie. Weekly, he would talk her out of her illusion that he was away because he wanted to be and that he was with another woman. He convinced Annie's doubts repeatedly that he was right there and would be there the moment his military orders released him.

Rosie's pregnancy was hard, as Annie's body fought her constantly. But she did not feel alone. Dimitri was there when she needed him. Just a phone call, FaceTime, or text away. They learned to communicate better and learned more and more about each other.

The more she learned, the more she liked it. Even now, she feels butterflies when she looks at him. His presence makes her feel calm, steady, and brave. Dimitri was able to get out of his deployment and hand off the lead position to the next rotation of men. He gave the officer all his connections and information, though when he took over, he was given nothing.

He worked hard to acquire those contacts and leads for training. At the end, he had worked with over ten countries militaries and had his men and him train with them. He was also invited to multiple conferences. He attended at times, and other times he had his men do it. Today he kept those contacts for when his squadron put out the money to go train, as he had.

He leaves the most exciting training to the younger guys to make them excited about joining the squadron. Anastasia was so amazed. In training, he and a few of his men were the only Americans and trained simultaneously with three other countries. All countries are friendly allies of America. To Anastasia, that was jaw-dropping information.

She giggled as he sent her sound clips, which she could not understand as people yelled in different languages. But she was so happy to have him back after eight long months. Mid-deployment, for Albert's second birthday, Dimitri flew Annie and Albert out to Poland. They spent a week and a half there, in different parts. They had such an amazing time.

Dimitri did still have to do some work while they were there. Anastasia brushed it off and embraced the fact that she had finally found a man who would do anything. Complete his schedule around seeing her and Albert. She felt lucky, and they used that time as a type of honeymoon. Dimitri chose hotels with separate room areas, so Albert did not see Dimitri and Anastasia as they slept and soaked in their love.

As he arrived home, Anastasia was nine months pregnant with Rosie. She was heavy and uncomfortable. She was nervous that Dimitri would not want her. He did not skip a beat. He was extraordinarily happy to be home with Annie and Albert.

They spent the last few weeks before Rosie came sleeping in Angus and Rose's basement. Then Rosie came, and Dimitri was changed forever. After nine months of buildup and eleven-hour of labor, he was finally able to hold his mini-me. Tears streamed down his face as he smiled and stared at her. He held her close and gently so as not to hurt her.

That day, Anastasia saw another shift in him. Different from the one she saw at the time they met and the time he met Albert. He was not just at home. He did not just have a purpose. But with the addition of Rosie, he knew he was set like wood that could not rot into the soil of this family.

Cement was constantly moving and was not made of natural components. But wood, like the trees, represented life, and the roots dug deep to look for their life source as their branches stretched high to connect to their other life source. They did not move as the wind swayed them; they just grew stronger and stronger. They certainly did not apologize for taking their space. Instead, they stood tall, confidently exposing their leaves to give them the sustenance they needed.

That day, Dimitri resembled the thirty five-year-old tree. Anastasia soaked up the moment, and then, thinking about it, she basked in the memory. I was reminding her of how far she had come and how lucky she was. It was not the same during Albert's pregnancy. The start was telling Chris he did not need to be responsible.

Then the rest was her working hard to provide and fighting to keep Albert happy and healthy. Rose held her hand, and Angus provided as they walked with her through her pregnancy. In the end, Chris had decided not to come to the birth. He requested not to be on the birth certificate. As she went into labor, after months of forced bed rest and having a dual stroke the day before, Angus rushed home to be with her.

Her water broke, and Rose told her to stay calm and try to relax. Her cousin told her to let her know when she was going to the hospital. Angus and Rose loaded up the car. Amber told Annie to eat a full meal and take a shower. Angus and Rose got Annie into the car and drove her to the hospital.

Anastasia labored for twenty-six hours total. Amber, Angus, and Rose stayed by her side amidst it all. When Albert was ready to arrive, it was Amber and Rose who held her feet. Unlike Rosie and Scott. Dimitri sat through labor with her, held her foot while she pushed, encouraged her, snuck her snacks, tried to tell her jokes, played games with her, and advocated for her.

Then, slept in the hospital with her until they could all leave together. This time was very different. Anastasia was so grateful for her cousin and parents, as they did whatever they could to be there for her. Angus cut Albert's umbilical cord. Dimitri cut both Rosie's and Scott's.

Anastasia spent that pregnancy without a mate. She spent the following three days being visited by her one friend, Amber, and her parents. Then they went home while Angus and Rose drove with Albert. Too small for his car seat, and too sick to truly cope with reality. At that time, Anastasia was so used to being left to be responsible for everything.

Rose felt akin to this and fiercely fought to make Anastasia feel as comforted, supported, and warm as possible, since Albert would not sleep. Rose would come down at four a.m. like clockwork and take Albert to the rocker so Anastasia could sleep. In many ways, it was Rose who saved Anastasia's and Albert's lives. God through Rose. She never looked at her like she was crazy; she asked, "What should we do now?"

Rose, Marie, and God worked to revitalize the dead inside Anastasia, encourage her, and build her up to be the mom Albert needed. Angus worked tirelessly to provide, and Rose watched Albert whenever Anastasia allowed her. The combination was a blessing. Anastasia punched herself for how she treated Amber and her, other family members at that time. She prayed God would forgive her and they would too, and he would give her the ability to forgive herself.

She had done so much wrong to Amber. She had apologized many times, but it never felt like enough. Though Amber was always fine with it and had forgiven her. "Time to forgive yourself, Annie. You no longer need to hold this piece. Everyone fails. Everyone hurts those around them, especially when they are hurting." A voice inside called out to her. Amber and Anastasia still talk from time to time.

The relationship was a sweet blessing. Anastasia would need more time to truly reach out and be okay with it all. Soon she would forgive herself enough to rekindle whatever the friendship would be. Or rest in the fact that Amber showed up for her in more ways than even her nuclear family.

At a time when Annie needed it most. Currently, Christmas cards and random texts. Anastasia was grateful and comfortable with this. One step at a time to healing.

Chapter Sixteen

Fly away, my love. You will not grow weary another day. Why was I so blinded by myself and didn't see you? How come I didn't spend more time with you? Now I am more, but is it enough?

Will I ever truly cry for you, my puppy, my dear? Where did the time go? How did we lose it all? twelve years for nothing—was it all worth it? I mourned for your death, and yet I seek to be comforted by you. What irony!

I wither in my seat while I think of the choices I've made and the ones I'm still making. When will I finally be free? Wait, when did this come to me? I seek to find you, and yet you cannot be found. I seek to hug you, yet you are not tangible.

I look into your eyes and think for a second that it is you. Then I realized it was a bulleted image. I long to pet you and watch you run around as you did when you were young. Why do I not cry? Is it because you are in a better place and, at least, not in pain?

Why did I not seek the chance to say goodbye one last time? Was it worth the wait, my love? Why can't I cry? Will I be able to escape this place I'm in? Is it now that defines our relationship and our time?

Will it linger? Please remove me, as you have been removed. Was it your time to go? Did we jump the gun? I had not even questioned our decision, but you knew, didn't you?

We all needed you and still do. You knew it would hurt. It's just too much to handle. Why is everything crashing in on me? Why can't I win?

A fool yet again. Why do I linger? Was that the point—to try? Is it me who desires to try alone? I am weak and not seeking help, and the help I do seek comes at a cost.

How come it is without malice that people feel it's so vital to debate every point? When I try to help, it only hurts. The guidance I give is cursed. Why do I stray? This is worth not crying about.

I am not only sad, but I am also angry. Don't allow it. I am confused. Release me. I feel trapped and lost. I feel like I have to make the decisions and take the steps.

But without you, I don't have knowledge or wisdom. Why have you left me? Why do you hide your face? Asking for clear guidance, yet you remain quiet. I cannot do this alone.

He is wrong for me. I get it. But why have you presented this? To show me how bad he is by showing me a godly man? Why?

I am so angry and confused. But I cannot be angry at you, God, because I fear you. Who do I get angry with? Myself? That creates more turmoil because I am an idiot.

I'm in Grade A, and I can't be angry at someone so stupid that they can't even function alone. So, who? Ian? Because he died? While this problem came about before his death and has continued after, he had nothing to do with it.

Albert? He may be ignorant, but he is not to blame for my benevolence. I blame the not-so-tangible fool inside of me. How could I let myself backtrack and hurt myself again?

Why am I destined for misery? I read, yes, but for nothing. I don't like this at all. Satan has hooked me, and now I am going for a ride. I just want to stay in the deep blue sea, where I can swim free.

And yet I wonder what it is like on land. He is totally land-ridden—a man by definition. And I am but a mermaid. We can never be together. Galatians thirty-one "Foolish Galatians. Who has bewitched you that you should not obey the truth, before whose eyes Jesus Christ was clearly portrayed among you as crucified?"

God answered to me about Albert, "Turn and run. It will only be pain and misery yet again."

How could I believe it would work this time? I didn't work before for a reason. It is not supposed to work. Thank you, God, you have answered me. I am finally ready to listen. Albert is out again, Anastasia thought back to a piece of writing that she had found days before. About a man she thought she loved before she met Chris.

This man was continuously supportive yet fervently adulterous. Though she loved Albert with her whole heart, she was reminded that she made the correct choice through this writing. That day, she had reached out to Albert through a social media interface. She wanted to let him know that she still thought about him and that she was still there for him if he needed her.

Albert did not reach back. Men rarely look to the past to find what their present and future needs are. Though the past will show you what the present and future will bring. Some things from the past do not need to be brought back to succeed and be happy in the present or future. People tend to take the same steps.

As Ecclesiastes states, "There is nothing new under the sun." Therefore, Anastasia liked to think back and look back at history to remind herself of what came before and what could come again. Obviously struggling to determine what was correct to bring out of her past and into her present and future. Annie always valued the most trivial things. She loved only a few people in her life, aside from her family.

Never let herself get too close to most people for fear of losing them or herself in some way. Albert, an old high school friend whom she loosely named her first son after, was one of those things. It had been years since they spoke. The most prominent time that plagued Annie to this day was when he was rotating home, and she blew up at him. If nothing else, this made her one of the worst people alive.

Who blows up at someone who is hanging on by a thread? Albert was patient and understanding but did not reach back unless necessary after that. Always being a little wiser than Annie. She explained, but her consciousness would not let it go. This was why she struggled to let him go.

Her heart yearned to be back in their town, walking around and chatting. Both have such different lives and are both in love with each other. Annie knew the only way to move forward in her current romance and love was to release herself of this wrong she had done and pray that God would be with Albert in every way. Only God knows what is best and perfect for each person. Only God knew what was truly in everyone's heart and mind.

A person could speak out what they believed to be the root of their actions and find out, after searching their mind and heart, it was not at all the case. Only God was perfect enough, insightful enough, wise enough, and knowledgeable enough to always know. Annie gave Albert to God and released him. She hoped he would have the best life possible and that all of his dreams would come true.

Chapter Seventeen

It was evening, and the kids ran and played inside. Outside, Dimitri shoveled snow from the porch as Anastasia sat back and struggled to focus. She thought of the many challenges that came her way and the ones that would continue to come. Last night was the first time in over nine months that she slept through the night without waking up for a baby. Though she felt the sting of hearing him cry in his crib, she knew this was the best option.

Scott had been extremely sick and struggled to breathe. Annie fought the anxiety inside, reminding her how fragile his life was. She knew she was doing what she could with what she had to help all her children heal from their sicknesses. It always felt overwhelming when the children were sick. It usually meant she and Dimitri were either going to get it in the middle of it or just getting over the same sickness.

When she was a kid, colds and flus traveled through her home the same way. Anastasia sat, grateful for a break from wrangling snot and fighting sickness. A moment where everyone was fine. She soaked up her moment to zone out. There was very little time for such pleasantries when a person had a new husband and three kids, four years of age and under. She stared at Albert and Rosie reading together and heard their little voices enjoying their time.

Scott seemed stuck in his Mission Impossible pose as he stared at Albert and Rosie, wishing he could be old enough to play with them. Just a year ago, Rosie sat and stared at Albert playing, as well. Anastasia hoped that in a year she would see all the kids sitting and reading together. Giving her even more free time and space. Dimitri, now in from shoveling, took the moment to exit the room and look at his phone.

It had been buzzing for the past few minutes from one of his multiple group chats. He was most certainly taking a moment to scan Instagram, which had become an addiction for him. Anastasia told herself to relax. Scanning a social media site and being a part of multiple group chats always had her worried. Instead of embracing the fear, she told herself Dimitri was a good man and only wanted to be with her.

It reminded her of the past. Social media and texting were big ways Chris connected with his ladies. He would not name his chats and would keep his phone hidden from Anastasia. On social media, he rarely added Annie to anything and got mad when she posted pictures of him. He did not want anyone to know he had a girlfriend.

It was easy for him to find people online before connecting to meet in person. When Annie was young, she had very little concern for such things. She knew Chris was always scraping by and needed to stay connected to many people. He was always selling things or buying things for cheap. At that time, Anastasia was convinced Chris was all hers.

It was not until a year or so into the relationship that she started to doubt. She asked, but he refused to tell her. She saw her fears flare for reasons unbeknownst to her. She considered asking because it worried her to see Chris not adding her to certain areas of his life. Yet when she spoke with him, he refused to explain to her.

He was scared she would catch him, and he would lose his back burner. This made Annie's red flags rise higher. She would dig deeper when the moment was right. When she tried in the past to cheat Chris, he just got angry to back her down. He would use attacks he knew worked to make her back off, letting him know she trusted him.

What trust can do for an honest person is make them strive to be more honest. What trust can do to a dishonest person is allow them to weasel out of their position and give them free access to whatever they want while you're not paying attention. Anastasia is still very much struggling with trust in men. She certainly had not been prepare for Dimitri to come along and had been so grateful for his deployment to ready herself for such a relationship. On their wedding day, her fears and emotions combined to break her down into a crying fit.

She did not want to be anyone's servant through life. Her marriage had become synonymous with death. Anastasia fought back her tears on that day as she stood in front of her family and married Dimitri. Since then, Annie's has seen what marriage really is: marriage to the right man. Marriage is a precious gift.

Every day you choose to love one person and devote your life to them, and they do the same. Each day is a chance to grow in love, trust, and respect. Dimitri has had to continue to be the strong and confident one. Anastasia felt his willpower dwindling in this area at times. He no longer wanted to have to fight so hard to keep her.

Now Anastasia needed to find out if she wanted and would stay of her own volition. It was not fair to the ever-constant Dimitri. He allowed her to face her fears and held her hand through them for years. But now he questioned if that was enough. She started to seek ways to help the family, and it sent red flags out.

He was scared that this meant she would leave him. It

seemed they had miscommunication. Their relationship had been extremely challenging; Annie would call it trial by fire. Four months, followed by an eight-month deployment. To a new baby and a chapel wedding two weeks later.

Then there was a one-year pandemic that still held on even two years later. Overly demanding friends and family. To try to not please people and be strong enough to make their own traditions. To another baby only a year after the second. To try to learn how to love and communicate with each other and with their children.

Realizing that though one income was working, maybe they could do better; maybe they could demolish all the debt they had acquired. Anastasia's CPTSD and crazy acts. Dimitri's wounds, two new cars, learning to maintain a household, and so on and so forth. They were sunk. Anastasia looked at Dimitri and saw how washed out and sickly he looked. She looked in the mirror and saw the same look on her face.

She considered that she had slept through the night for the first time and wanted that to fix everything. Tomorrow Dimitri would go back to his overly demanding job, and again, new pressure would be added to the well-oiled dynamic they had. She was so grateful for his job but hated how he was treated. She hated that the other men saw Dimitri as the guy who got things done. It made him be away for more hours and carry more weight than anyone should have to bear alone.

A weight so heavy at work did not stop the demands at home. Anastasia's heart hurt for him, and she wanted to help him in any way possible. She prayed God would teach her how to be his helpmate, and she just kept showing up for him. She knew one thing was certain. She wanted to be married to and love this man.

She could not escape the past she needed so badly to heal

from. Even that was part of her, and if he loved her, he would take it too. Holding her hand while she healed. She took a deep breath, finding her solution, and quietly got up from the couch and went into the other room. She found Dimitri still on his phone, zoned out, scrolling. She looked away from his phone and hugged him.

The emotion was too much for her as Dimitri put his phone down and hugged her tightly, so she started making jokes. Annie moved her hands from the small of his back to his back pockets. She squeezed and giggled. Dimitri giggled too as he rolled his eyes and said, "Little eyes are watching." Annie looked over at their kids still playing in the other room and zeroed in on Dimitri.

Now she hugged him tighter and laid her head on his chest. "I just wanted to love you a little, but while you are home. I am going to miss you tomorrow when you go back."

"I have been home for five days and will only be at work for a few days. You will be fine."

What Dimitri failed to let himself see is that if he just listened for a moment and did not try to protect Anastasia, he would hear that she loved him. This was overall his biggest fear. The fear that she would leave when things got hard or that she would find something better was all tied into the fear that he was unworthy of her love and incapable of being loved. Annie and Dimitri shared this fear; this was a strong bond Anastasia knew they had. Both are gorgeous and so easy to love.

They had both been marred by the past. From hurt people, they were told they could not be loved and shown such things. They did not love those hurting people, and those people flung it back on them. For Annie,, it had been a few guys but mostly Chris. For Dimitri, it had been his previous ex's: Tabetha, Stephanie, and Claire.

In their own ways, they convinced him that he was not enough. So he began to believe it. Anastasia whispered, "I want you."

Dimitri said, "Save it for later." Anastasia again

"No, I want you. Dimitri. You are my miracle man and one true love." Dimitri blew it off. He hugged Anastasia, then went to check on the mellow children.

He hugged Albert as he screamed, "Stop, Dad!"

"But I love hugs," replied Dimitri. Albert and Dimitri had a weird dynamic. Anastasia could see the strain in Dimitri as he played it off. He wanted Albert to learn boundaries, so he showed him what he was doing to others.

But I also really needed Albert's love. He thought it was still integral to Annie's love for him. Anastasia already knew Albert was safe and happy with Dimitri, and that was enough for her. Dimitri also took it upon himself to teach Albert many traits and respect for others, which Albert, who had always been served, had struggled with. Overall, their bond was much more than a hug here and there. It was an unspoken, unbreakable bond that Dimitri, Albert, and Anastasia knew would last a lifetime.

Chapter Eighteen

In the morning, after saying goodbye to Dimitri, feeding the children, doing home school, and making sure everyone had what they needed, Anastasia got caught on her phone. She scrolled through the main feed of a popular site. She came upon a new business she had not seen before. A tree farm an old friend owned. She scrolled through the pages and took a screenshot of Chris.

As that was the family, he decided he most wanted to be like early on. He was attached to the son and tried to learn from his dad. The father had been a farmer all of his life. When he was a kid, it was a cattle farm. As an adult, he and his wife ran a construction company and lived on land that no longer supported cattle.

However, in his free time, he would make money doing anything he could. Mostly hunting and trapping. His wife was a good Christian country woman. She made meals and kept the house when she was not at work. Together, they kept up a genuine country life.

During off-weeks, the father would take the kids to the south to hunt. He raised two children who loved to hunt and work. They rarely had time for television or anything to do with entertainment. Unlike the rest of American society, they lived out every minute. Anastasia had heard that both the children got married.

She had no idea that the daughter had started the tree farm.

She loved the family and silently cheered for Hannah as she scrolled through the pictures. It was not long ago that she and Hannah had a real bond. Hannah reminded Anastasia a lot of herself. But Hannah was overall more confident and much more of a go-getter.

When Annie visited Hannah's family with Chris, it usually ended up that Chris would go with her brother and Annie would go with Hannah. Anastasia hated how she had left things. She forgot to return some clothes she borrowed. She spent a night at their house with Chris and walked through the house naked, thinking she could salvage the broken relationship with Chris. The family had been away, and Chris was house-sitting.

During the day, they walked the land. Chris showed Annie his campground and tried to convince her to camp instead of going back to the house to sleep. She commented on how cold it was. There was snow and ice everywhere on that December day. Chris explained that winter camping was the best because they could keep each other warm.

Anastasia wished to appease him, but after walking the woods all day, she wanted a warm house to rest in. It was the day that Chris thought it best to walk through and hunt. He had two shotguns with him. He thought it would be fun to hunt chipmunks. At one point, he saw a chipmunk running.

He tossed his shotgun to Annie, then ran and posted. He watched the chipmunk and then banged. The chipmunk, once in full stride, is now lying on the floor of the woods. Chris had hit it in the heart. These were the moments he tried to impress Annie.

He looked back at her, knowing she could do the same. She asked if she should take a turn, to which his face of pride fell, and he said, "Let's move on and cook this up." That evening, they left the chipmunk at the camp to stay cold as they went back to

Hannah's empty house. In the morning, Anastasia cooked some bacon for Chris. Like most men, Chris loved bacon.

It was not until a week or so later that she found out she was not the only girl he had invited over that week. She was crushed but realized this was his MO, and if she wanted him, she would have to give up the illusion she was the only one. Though she did nothing horrible, walking through the house naked always made her feel gross. Why would she do such a thing in someone else's house? Empty or not.

It was wrong of her. Especially for a guy who did not deserve such things. After a few years, Anastasia was sent out on a mission to get self-rising flour for the Chinese food restaurant. Anastasia went to four different Walmarts and found very few. By the end of her search, she was within an hour of needing to go to the restaurant.

She grabbed some food after not eating all day. Anastasia was extremely grumpy and recently found out she was pregnant with Albert. As she was cashing out, Hannah came and stood beside her. Anastasia was deflated, exhausted, late, and extremely hungry. Hannah was young, lively, and bubbly.

I was so excited to see Annie in her neck of the woods. But Anastasia refused to look up. She refused to interact. She was angry and embarrassed. So instead of engaging, she just kept her head down and walked away.

She headed to her car and gobbled up her food, considering how rude she had been. I was trying to figure out who would be so excited to see her. She landed on it; it certainly needed to be Hannah, but for years she refused to let herself off the hook. It was time Anastasia released herself from such things. It's not like we can go back and fix things.

The past is written. The present is meant to be lived, and the future is to come. But still, she felt she had been wronged by the family, so she liked the page and considered buying something. But as she scrolled through the few years' worth of pictures, Anastasia saw a few with Chris in them.

She knew that even though she loved this family deeply, it was not her place. She had grown to deeply love all the people Chris posted around her. She spent most of her adult years trying to take care of them in the best way she could. Those people took care of her and looked after her. There was a deep bond.

But when Anastasia had Albert, those who disapproved during the pregnancy wrote her off. Those who held on after were all connected to Chris. Some even fought for her as Chris brought other women around. They did not understand or know how much Anastasia loved Chris and was willing to fight for their relationship. She looked at these pictures.

How he has changed, she thought. Long hair, long beard. Basically, trying to look like a different person. He never wanted pictures of his face and always contorted it. Much like Albert does now to make others laugh.

For Chris, it was to make his face untraceable. Anastasia thought he was certainly untraceable now. She knew he had many motives for this; Chris always had many underwriting of motives. He started working for his dad's business at a very young age. Always training to be better, always running from the bad people like the kid in kindergarten.

Though in his adult years, Anastasia watched as he transformed into those bad people. She tried to hold him back, but he hurt her as he mutated from this pleasant person into the people he feared the most. Anastasia watched one transformation, and as she had to raise Albert, she prayed she would not have to watch another one. She knew what was in his blood.

She knew she and Chris had become sociopaths and had done unspeakable things. She knew during her pregnancy in Albert's first year of life that she spent countless hours reversing the mental games she played to survive in such a life. Taking her from Harley Quinn back to a pleasant and loving Anastasia. She knew she had skills no one would ever consider her having, and she knew that Chris was the reason for many of them. Always trying to teach her how to defend herself from bad people but using herself as his very own punching bag.

As his caged animal to unleash when he pleased. Anastasia felt the love in her heart for Hannah and her family, but she could not go back. She could not reveal that side of herself to Dimitri and the kids. She certainly could not put them through that hell. To this day, Anastasia stayed away from situations where she needed to use her special skills.

She feared what would happen if she unleashed her dragon in front of those she loved. They would certainly fear her and look at her differently. So, she held it inside and calmed it as the urge arose. She spent too much time reminding herself that if she wanted her family and a good life, she must only use her dragon when it really counts. I reminded Dimitri once again that if Chris came, he should take the kids and run, and she would handle it.

Though Dimitri was strong, he did not have the mind of a sociopath. He called himself crazy, but Anastasia knew it wasn't true. It takes being crazy to recognize it. And she saw nothing of the sort. In order to keep her dragon inside and her family together at this point, she needed to completely release her old friend groups.

Moments would arise where she would reach out, but they were few and with little follow-through. Ultimately, she knew the only way she could protect her family was to start over completely. She kept her own family close—parents and siblings. But anyone connected to Chris was pushed out of her life. With Dimitri, she was happy.

Though it had proven to be extremely challenging to make a new friend group at this new home, at this time in her life, she held out hope that one day she would have a group of women to visit and share a life with. One day, it would all work out. Not today, but someday soon. Until then, she would focus all her efforts on the family and miracles God gave her, and the purpose and charge were set before her. That would be more than enough.

Finally able to build on her own life and set in quiet to heal from the years she spent building others up. Anastasia's vision of the past faded as she twirled her hair and took deep breaths, trying to release the guilt she felt toward Gressinger's. They were trying to rejoice in the fact that they were doing so well. She looked up at the beautiful land in front of her house. Barren trees with layers of sparkling white snow surrounding them.

She saw the houses a mile away in between her and the houses amongst the field covered in snow. She saw what she deemed a sign. She saw a flock of geese munching on the sprigs that stuck through the snow. Those geese had been eating from the land on and off for the past few days. Did you know geese mate for life?

They find their one goose, and they stay with them until they are parted by death. It was in this fact that Annie found solace. She realized God was showing her what he had constantly told her. He was showing her that she and Dimitri were like geese. They would be together until death or God parted them.

Nothing else could ever move them. Both are so stubborn and grouchy. They both sought God to better each other's lives.

They both wanted to be married and raise a happy family. Also known as, their goals for the future are aligned.

Anastasia knew somehow, some way Dimitri and her would build an empire to help them live a godly life and to glorify their God. They were a long way off, but they were taking steps every day. Dimitri even started to fix up the house slowly. He added rugs, organizers, and a new closet bar to give Anastasia more space. Almost two years into their marriage, it took him to face the closet.

But last night, sure enough, though it was an overwhelming challenge, he did it. Anastasia took every opportunity to thank and encourage him. She saw him facing a fear head on, and she rejoiced that he allowed her in so much, especially with the added benefit of giving her more space. As he started to panic, she calmly moved some items to her side and gave him bins until he got a shelf and bookcase in the closet. Even the bar was huge.

She stood and planned with him. He decided on his own to purge in the future. But Anastasia reassured him that there was no rush. She reaffirmed that this was his project, and she would not get in the way or push. He let her purge and organize the entire house.

The least she could do would be to give him his closet. She saw her face in relief, and they smiled and hugged. "Well, now that that is done, shall we go for a lovely moonlit walk on the farm?" Dimitri asked.

Anastasia smiled and said, "Sure!"

They enjoyed traipsing through the snow, holding hands, and chatting like little kids. At the top of a hill on their property, Dimitri stopped and turned around. Annie followed his lead. They both took deep breaths and stared at the splendor God had created and given to them to steward over. Out of breath fell.

Again, in, then out. They both breathed out their fears and anxieties. They breathed in the moment of beauty together to replace what came out through their breathing. Soon it was too cold, and they hurried inside. One more night together was a blessing only God could allow, as Dimitri was not supposed to be home this week. They held hands as they fell asleep beside each other after Anastasia thanked him one more time and kissed his cheek.

Chapter Nineteen

Dimitri worked hard as he tried to tie the squadron he was currently working for together. He came home and let Anastasia know that he had loosely volunteered for a four-month deployment over the holidays the following year. Anastasia took deep breaths quietly as, at times, Dimitri said things to see her reaction. He had learned this trait from his current boss. She had seen a lot of his current boss come out in him at times.

It always made her wonder if it was actually who he described his boss to be. Though when they were home together for more than a few days, she saw the true Dimitri shine through and once again felt confident she had made the right choice. Dimitri's boss, Carl, was a narcissist. He had spent his life convincing people around him in the way he wanted to get what he wanted. He was a master of mind games.

Anastasia had also become a master at such mind games and therefore spent an abundant amount of time explaining to Dimitri how to handle such a man. Though she was wrong at times, she was usually right. Functioning at a high-mind game, read through people's lies and see right into the core of each person. It did not hurt that she was beautiful and lovely to be around, always complimenting people. She did such things to pull the information she needed in a limited time, trying to do such things somewhere in life.

Ultimately, Dimitri was using the same mind games on Anastasia to see how she would react so he could understand how he should react. Anastasia stayed calm and quiet for a moment. She told him he could go if he wanted to, but he would need to make her pregnant again before he left. Dimitri half smiled, then said, "Well, I don't want to go. I am still in my dwell time, so they cannot make me go. So, I will volunteer for next year if they are still running the deployment." Anastasia reiterated that she did not mind.

To which Dimitri replied, "No, I want to stay home with you guys." They sat and ate their meal that Dimitri had slow-cooked, and Anastasia plated. Soon Rosie decided she was done and got down from her stool.

Scott stared as she played, and Albert finished his plate and got down to go play. They started with Albert ripping the toy from Rosie's hand and Rosie screaming a high-pitched eagle like scream. Dimitri caught on and yelled at Albert to give it back and apologize. Albert did so begrudgingly. Then I grabbed a different toy.

Rosie kept playing. Dimitri looked at Anastasia. "Off to a great start." Annie rolled her eyes and smiled. Scott begged for more of his pureed beans with apples and pulled pork. He loved to eat.

Anastasia fed him a few more spoonfuls, then started to clean the kitchen. Taking breaks to feed him more, he asked with a whiny grunting noise. He looked as though he was grabbing a motorcycle as he begged for another bite. It made Anastasia giggle and want to feed him. This evening, she flashed back through her motorcycle memories.

When she was young, her dad bought a motorcycle from the junkyard and fixed it up. He would take them all on rides through town, and Anastasia loved it. As she got older, Angus got some used dirt bikes for Annie and her siblings. They learned to drive them after a while. Angus wanted to teach them to drive everything they could.

Anastasia even rode dirt bikes on ice one frozen day. However it all came to a halt after she had a friend ride on the back and stick her leg in the back wheel. That friend broke her leg, and Anastasia was lucky she did not get sued. After that, she rarely drove motorcycles or dirt bikes. The years would go by, and she would go on the motorcycle with her dad only for rides.

It was not until she met Chris that she rode on anyone else's motorcycle. Chris was involved with a dirt bike racket. He would buy beat-down dirt bikes, fix them up, and then sell them for a couple thousand more than he bought them. She rode on his dirt bikes and motorcycles a lot. One time, she rode with shorts and a tank top.

She came home to her father screaming at her before she even got off the bike. "Never do that again. You know what the road would do to you if you crashed? You wear layers on a motorcycle. I never want to see this again."

Chris agreed after he was the one who urged her to wear that outfit. But in front of Angus, he wanted to look like a good guy. The memory that stood out most to Anastasia was her and Chris's first official date. He asked to meet her and Marie at the bowling alley. It was a summer evening, and they came to find out he was not alone.

They found he had brought friends. Being polite, Annie and Marie went around and greeted the group individually. Anastasia came to a guy who, when she shook his hand, said, "Now we can never marry because you touched my hand." Anastasia was taken aback. All she could think was, I am here with your friend, and you are talking to me about marrying you.

Good I may want to marry your friend, but I will not even

dream of marrying you. They would go on to become friends, but not once would it cross Anastasia's mind to marry him. Chris had another friend from this group who begged and pleaded for Annie and Marie's numbers. He told Chris, "I will pay you $500 for one of their numbers." Chris refused and told Annie and Marie to stay away from him, and he should stay away from them.

Annie would also become friends with this guy, and he would come to help her in many ways. I never thought Anastasia or Marie would hang out with him without Chris present. Bowling was boring as always, thought Anastasia. But then the group all went outside, and Chris gave Annie and Marie rides on the dirt bike. They all had a blast.

Soon it was late, and the bowling alley closed. So Chris told them to follow him to the park. Though the park was gated, they entered. They lay on the grass and stared at the stars. This was the park Anastasia went to and her family would go watch fireworks in the future.

It was a starry night that lacked fireworks in all regards. Soon, the cops saw their cars and came to check them out. Anastasia did not like cops from the past and told Chris they should run. Chris really liked this aspect, which meant she would not call the cops on him even if he did things unheard of. He told her, "No, we should go talk to them. They probably just want us to leave the park. It's not a big deal. See Marie and my buddy are already talking with them, let's go." They gave the group a warning and waited until they got in their vehicles and left. The night ended like that.

They said their goodbyes and went to their individual homes. Chris would have Anastasia go back to that rundown bowling alley repeatedly throughout their relationship; she never would have liked it. The last day, she let him force her there. She got so angry because he was flirting with other girls that she would take herself outside to throw herself against the snowbank until the pain stopped. She had become accustomed to being masochistic so as not to hurt others to the best of her ability.

Chris came out and fought with her. They went back to the group as Chris guilted her into it, and she had no vehicle to go home. At the end of the night, all those friends went outside and had a huge snowball fight in the parking lot. Anastasia marked it as one of her lowest and highest moments within that friend group. Years would go by, and she would drive by once in a while, thinking of all those glimpses of memories.

She heard a whining noise again as she sank back into reality. In front of her was her precious Scott, revving his little hands and looking at her intensely and whining for more. She dipped the spoon in his puree and gave him another bite. Drifting between the two worlds for a bit longer she realized she needed to come back to reality.

Anastasia started looking around and taking deep breaths in and out. She saw the fridge, her son, her Dimitri, and the older kids playing. She yearned to be present. After more deep breaths, she felt the chair under her, supporting her weight.

She felt one of her hands resting on her leg, the other arm was poised to give Scott another bite mindlessly. The picture that surrounded her got louder and louder until she came back to it. Forgiving and forgetting so she could truly be present with her miracles was her goal. Dimitri cracked a joke, and Annie came back just in time to catch it.

She started witty banter with him and brought Scott into the playroom after wiping him off. He smiled and squealed with delight as he watched his siblings play and tried to join. Anastasia smiled and knew she was right where she was meant to be.

Chapter Twenty

It was an uninspired day as Anastasia looked after the kids. She fed them, clothed them, schooled them, read to them, played with them, and made them brush their teeth in her. She felt the pain in her body, causing her head to spin and her to come in and out of the world of illusion. Anastasia rarely ever truly felt pain in her abdomen. Usually, she only knew she was in pain because her body would lash out in different ways.

Earlier that morning, as she fed Scott, she felt a solid, hard item in her abdomen. She massaged her abdomen, hoping to move it along and break it up a bit. At that time, she felt no pain. Though as the day progressed, so did the sign that her body was in distress. Her abdomen did not give these signs, as it had become completely numb over the years.

When she was a child, Annie found herself to have a high pain threshold. She later found that this coincided with warrior blood. Through her years, many things that would hurt and break others rarely affected her. When she was with Chris, she found the same theme. Though this time, her body did push to breaking.

She found herself so sick that she would go into shock on the first day of her period. She was so sick that she could not stand for more than ten minutes at a time, and when she tried; her body would start to fall over. One day, at the peak of her distress, she was at work. Anastasia graded clothes for a secondhand store. Only she was in the room between the bars, like always.

Everything was fine until her peripheral picked up

something eye-level with her. She turned her head to look. It was the bar that normally stood shoulder height with her now at her cheek. The bars stayed solidly in one place as the structure was formed in such a way. Annie soon realized she thought she was standing, though she had actually been falling over.

She went into the break room to sit down. Her abdomen had been in excruciating pain for what seemed to be weeks. Only a few days later, the pain ramped up, and Annie thought to leave work only to realize she did not have the strength to get to her car. She knew if she walked that far, her legs would give out and it would make a scene, so she went to sit in the break room until she had the strength to stand again.

Once more, Anastasia was on a long walk in California with Rose. They traveled to watch over Rose's mom (Annie's grandma) after surgery. While she rested, Rose and Annie took their walk across town. They walked through the neighborhoods that connected Annie's grandma's apartment building with the main drag of the town. It took them an hour in each direction.

They stopped once for Rose to go to the bathroom. "Do you need to go as well, Annie?" asks Rose.

"No, I will just wait outside. Thank you."

Anastasia sat down and waited outside. When she tried to get back up, her body refused to allow her. She sat there, feeling paralyzed. Realizing Rose would know something was wrong; Annie tried to will herself to stand up. When this did not work, she started to pray vigorously so that she could stand when Rose came out of her bathroom break.

Sure, enough Rose appeared at the door. Anastasia smiled and used all her strength to stand. God must have lifted her that day because she knew it was not her own broken-down body. Those days, Anastasia worked hard and slept very little. Usually, she worked two to three jobs to support her and Chris.

When she got out, Chris forced her to go hang out with friends, and then he would only allow her four hours of sleep. Most of those nights, she slept in her car, as it made little sense to drive an hour and a half of those hours to sleep in a bed. Anastasia worked and worked, but she never had enough money. She cleaned and cleaned, but Chris would not allow that; he trashed her things. He wanted to remind her that he controlled her and she was dirt.

Anastasia figured all men would be like that and wanted so badly to be good enough for Chris. So she took each lash, and the moments he criticized her, she explained to him that she could do better. She worked harder and harder to be good enough for him. But it was never enough. He was never satisfied.

Always a snide comment or him reminding her of her place. Anastasia was so innocent and new to relationships, but she knew things were not right. She strove for a time so they could be together more and live in one house. That is why Chris kept using up her money. He did not want any of that to happen, and he knew Annie would freely give it to him.

Anastasia became too sick. She was killing herself from the inside. She was no longer human. The way her brain worked was to please and worship Chris because maybe one day he would treat her better. She made him her obsession.

She could give up anything but him. Along the way, many people tried to help Annie, but Chris played the victim, and Anastasia felt she needed to protect him from those people who we're trying to protect her. She brushed them aside and worshipped him. Now he had her all and used it to let her know she was nothing but the poop on his shoes he liked to stomp on and forcefully scrape off. Have any of you had anyone treat you in such a way?

Anastasia blamed herself for many things she had never done wrong. As she lay beside Dimitri and confessed to him the wrong, she felt she was doing it, even though she could feel that her mind was stacked against her. "I'm a bad mom because Scott had a poor reaction to the rescue remedy. I gave it to him to help him survive the sickness. I'm a bad person because when I stood in front of everyone singing, I failed and disturbed their worship.

I'm a bad person because seven years ago I said this one thing to this person, and it hurt their feelings." The words left her mouth, and they hit her. First off, these are people she no longer interacts with. Secondly, they likely have no memory of such things and probably remember other parts of the event. Thirdly, how does doing human things make her a bad person?

Anastasia felt guilty for holding these things in and allowing them to hold her back. It was hard to explain why she rarely acted human, even years later. Someone did something uncomfortable or that she could not control, and she left the room to give them privacy with no words. They spoke with her, and instead of going to her screaming child, she so desperately wanted to help. She needed to sit and listen to the stories she did not even care about.

What would happen if she did not? In her mind, every situation or scenario was dangerous. She could not even recall a situation. Chris did not find a way to punish her for just being present. He told her the things he did not like about her. He attacked her for talking to anyone, and he made her look like a fool in front of anyone and everyone he could.

If he did not, then she would shine. Anastasia saw herself exhibiting the same habits as Dimitri from time to time. Lacking the ability to heal, she attacked him in the same way. Any woman was around, and she attacked Dimitri. His family or friends were around, and she made a fool of herself at times, which embarrassed them both.

But I mainly tried to do what was best in those situations. Her heart and soul wanted to lift Dimitri up, to trust and love him. But her mind was poisonous. She knew going into their relationship meant she had a lot of healing to do. She knew only he could truly enter into a marriage with her.

Dimitri had been through a tough life, and Anastasia saw his stubbornness and warrior blood. He matched her in every way. She knew letting him go would be the greatest mistake of her life. But now she saw that she was conditioning him to be fearful of being around others. There were moments when he begged her on.

There were moments when she saw in him a guy who was all she feared. "It's so easy to cheat on a stay-at-home mom." Enter a room, and he would look at everyone and say, "I am just making sure we are safe. I need to make sure there are no threats."

Logically, this was a lot for a man, but to a jaded woman, this meant only one thing. He was looking for the next best option. Anastasia feared most when Dimitri was around other women. It was her mind and heart that created the challenge. Even in a room filled with men, the fear inside her raged.

She considered the option of him wanting other men in a world that bombarded us with such options. So she would get uncomfortable in any setting, which made Dimitri uncomfortable. He knew he could not go anywhere without a comment from Annie. "I bet you liked her butt. I saw the way you looked at him."

Reader, if your mind or someone else's mind is playing tricks on them like this, you can be assured this is a spiritual attack. Instead of zeroing in on the specific attacks, it is best to open your mind to the God of the universe. She continually thought, *Am I with another Chris? Are all men pigs at times?* She came to resolve, in her worst moments, that she would raise the kids with him no matter what.

Then, if he was the way she saw him in those moments, she would ask to leave. Asking meant telling. But at the best moments, when she was sure he was all hers, she knew they could grow old together. Annie struggled back and forth. She fought off each side day in and day out.

Things she certainly would not notice as a working mom. But as a stay-at-home mom, she saw it all and analyzed it to nauseum. Everything came down to what Anastasia wanted. Men will be men. He will cheat, no matter the circumstances, if that is what he wants to do.

He will use those bar trips for more than time with guys. He expressed that he goes to work out early and uses it to sleep with women. People around her would continue to look at her like she was crazy. She would continue to force an overactive sexual relationship on him in hopes he would stay faithful. But when did it all end?

When would it be enough for her to just settle into the relationship? With Chris, she settled in easily. But Dimitri has always been ready to let go if the need presented itself. Why? Dimitri showed up more, and love bombed less.

He was curmudgeony and stubborn. Chris was great at romance but sucked at showing up. Which was love? What type of love did Anastasia desire? Obviously, more romance was necessary with Dimitri.

But the other parts were better than anyone she had been with. Anastasia felt at war inside. A weak day, she thought as she recapped the times Dimitri failed to fully explain, and when he did explain, Annie failed to absorb it. Anastasia was done searching. She decided to grow her family with this man.

The good, the bad, and the ugly—she signed on for all of this with Dimitri when she said her vows. At the end of her debate, one truth remained. Dimitri and Anastasia would hurt each other, fight, and even betray each other. That is what humans do. Especially humans who are married for life.

No one else was beside her in her vision of her old age. Dimitri made Annie less worried about old age. She saw an old, grayed Greek man in a rocker on their porch, his cane staring out at the land. Now she thought how do I get from here to there? A small voice came from her gut. "Settle in, Annie. It's time to settle in."

Annie felt peace with these words, and tears came to her eyes. *That's right,* she thought, *It's time. Finally, time. I know what I want, and it is Dimitri, no matter what. I want to grow old with Dimitri and fight through life with him. No longer will the fear of him cheating or leaving me find me. I have made up my mind. Now I need to truly live by it. Not just play wife.* But she fell into the role of Dimitri's wife. *Just as I am, it's time. Fail, as I might and likely will. I most certainly will fall flat on my face, and if he loves me, he will too. That is the name of the game."*

Annie wrote to Dimitri, "You were right, you know. I have been holding back, thinking this could end at any moment. Always on my toes. But even with that, you have become my constant. Every day, I'm scared.

"Every day I fight to face this fear of being with you and having our family. I am so scared you will become abusive or a cheater. I am so scared I won't catch it. I am scared that when my life falls apart again, you will be the one who makes it happen. Fighting fears is exhausting, and I want to lay into our love.

"To release my breath and finally relax. I know none of the attacks in my mind are true. Even if it is, it does not matter, because I chose you to build a family with whom to grow old. It's daily that I dream of being on a battlefield and being able to use physical skills to fight off the enemy or die. So, I no longer have to suffer.

"But I was born for spiritual and mental battles, mainly. You were mainly born for physical battle, I think."

Dimitri replied, "We are fine, babe; we are all under our own unique stress and problems."

Anastasia continued, "I love you. I have failed, am failing, and will always fail you.

But when you wake up each morning, I will be there. That is what I can offer you. What can you offer me?"

Dimitri responded, "I love you as well, my beautiful wife. I offer you my unwavering love and support."

Something so simple yet so profound, Anastasia thought straight to the point.

She responded to Dimitri, "Thank you."